The Mountain of Magic

The battle between good and evil begun in *The Tree that Sat Down* and *The Stream that Stood Still* comes to a dramatic climax in the final volume of Beverley Nichols's fantasy trilogy. Jill and her brother Jack set out on an expedition to the mountain of magic and are pursued by Sam and the witch Miss Smith, who are determined to get their final revenge and destroy the children.

D0999301

Here are some more fantasy stories to thrill you:

Beverley Nichols

The Mountain of Magic

Illustrated by Peggy Fortnum

Lions

First published by Jonathan Cape Ltd in 1950
First published in this abridged edition in Lions 1975
Ninth impression July 1991

Lions is an imprint of the Children's Division,
part of HarperCollins Publishers Ltd,
77–85 Fulham Palace Road,
Hammersmith, London W6 8JB

Copyright (abridged edition) © Beverley Nichols 1975

ISBN 0 00 671027-1

The author asserts the moral right to be
identified as the author of this work.

Printed and bound in Great Britain by
HarperCollins Manufacturing, Glasgow

Conditions of Sale
This book is sold subject to the condition
that it shall not, by way of trade or otherwise,
be lent, re-sold, hired out or otherwise circulated
without the publisher's prior consent in any form of
binding or cover other than that in which it is
published and without a similar condition
including this condition being imposed
on the subsequent purchaser

Dedicated to my young friend
ROB STUART
in the fond hope that he will
always take after his mother
and
the happy assurance that he
already takes after his grandfather

1. The Adventure Begins

When Jack woke up that morning he knew that something very wonderful and very special was going to happen, but for the moment he was too sleepy to remember what it was.

He lay there in the huge bed, with its gold crown glittering high above him, blinking lazily at the sunshine that flooded through the silken curtains. Then, all of a sudden, he noticed something which made him feel wide awake in an instant, and caused him to jump out of bed in a single leap.

It was a pair of spiked shoes lying on the window-ledge, the shoes with which he hoped to climb the steepest cliffs that any boy had ever climbed.

And today – how could he ever have forgotten it, even for an instant? – today was the great day on which he and Jill were going to set out for the Magic Mountain.

He tiptoed over to the window, and sat down to try on the shoes for the hundredth time. Yes, they fitted beautifully, and the spikes were so sharp that he longed to put them to the test that very minute. However, when he had started to climb the main staircase last night, his mother had been very annoyed and had told him that he would make holes in the carpet. So he supposed he would have to wait.

He sighed, drew back the curtains, and looked out. The great clock on the watch-tower told him that it was only ten minutes to six. The Palace was asleep. The only sound came from the cooing of the doves and the plash of the fountains far below. Even the three white peacocks had not yet begun to strut about, but stayed very still by the lily pond, lost in the dreams that peacocks dream – which, of course, are all of vanity and of the things of this world.

He gave a long, low whistle. One of the peacocks heard it, looked up and saw him. This bird nudged his two companions, who also looked up. Then, very grandly, and very gracefully, all three of them rose, slowly spread their tails and bowed. When they had done this they all gave a very meaning glance towards the Palace clock, and sat down again. They were not going to say anything – oh no! They knew their place. But they were not used to being woken so early, even by a Prince.

Jack waved to them, turned back into the room, and tiptoed over to the other great bed, where his sister lay sleeping.

'Jill! Jill! Wake up!'

Slowly she opened her eyes and stared at him.

'What is it?'

'It's the day! The day we go to the Mountain!'

She sat up with a start. 'Heavens! Are we late?'

'No. It's only just six o'clock. But I *can't* wait any longer.'

Jill knew that as she was the elder of the two she ought to tell her brother not to be silly, but to go back to bed for another hour. But she too felt something which made her long to get up at once.

'I'll run down and see that everything's all right with the donkey cart,' suggested Jack.

And before she could say another word, he had darted

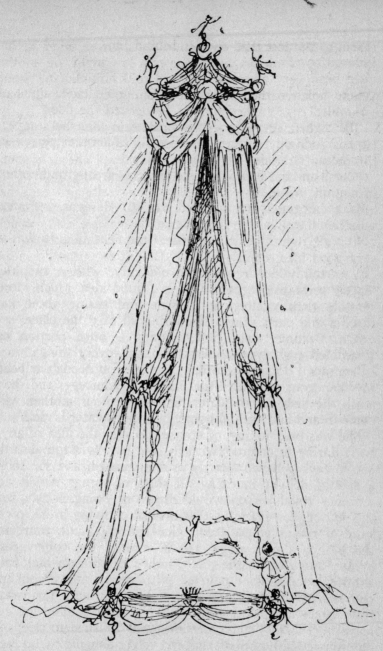

Tiptoed over to the other great bed

through the door and shut it behind him.

*

When Jack returned to the bedroom, a delicious smell of scrambled eggs greeted him as he opened the door.

'Jill!' he cried, running forward. And then he stopped. He had suddenly noticed that there was another person in the room. 'Grannie! I'd no idea . . .'

'Come and eat your eggs,' snapped his great-grandmother in a gruff voice.

Jack hesitated and glanced at Jill. He was not sure whether they were in disgrace.

'It's all right, Jack,' said Jill. 'Grannie thinks it was a very good idea, don't you?'

'I certainly do,' replied the old lady, with a twinkle. 'Eating scrambled eggs is always a good idea. Much more sensible than putting on crowns and sitting about on thrones and curtseying and saluting all over the place.'

'Oh, Grannie,' said Jack, gulping a huge portion of scrambled eggs, 'you do say the most lovely things.'

'Perhaps I do,' she retorted, 'though you needn't tell me so when your mouth is full. Finish up your eggs and then wash the dish in hot water. Otherwise your mother will come in and find us, and I shall be in hot water myself.'

She was only joking, of course, because the idea of any-body daring to be cross with the old lady was too absurd. She always behaved exactly as she wanted, and she took a special delight in doing all sorts of things which no ordinary royal person would dream of doing. It was for this reason, for example, that instead of living in her own suite of rooms at the Palace she had chosen to retire to the branches of a huge tree in one of the courtyards. Winter and summer she stayed in her lofty nest, which had a little wooden floor covered with rushes and a roof of common straw. Very cosy it was, too, up there, far away from everybody, and nothing would ever induce her to leave it. 'I should suffocate,' she said, 'if I had to sleep in an ordinary bed, with all that red velvet hanging round me. What's more, I should forget how to work any magic.'

4

This was, indeed, the real reason why she was so fond of living up in the branches of the tree, all by herself. In her old age she had grown more and more fascinated by magic; she had a whole shelf of ancient books on the subject, and an old chest full of strange powders and rare chemicals, with which she was in the habit of experimenting. Sometimes late at night if you had happened to be wandering in the courtyard near Grannie's tree, you might quite likely have heard a small explosion, followed by puffs of smoke of a most repulsive smell, and if you had not known what it was you might well have imagined that some sort of war was beginning between somebody or other. But it would only have been Grannie, trying out her magic.

The King was often very worried about these goings-on, particularly when the smells were extra bad and were blowing through his window.

'I know you'll blow yourself up one of these days,' he used to say.

To which the old lady would retort that he was talking nonsense. And she would drop a dark hint that one of these days they might all be very grateful that she had been working so hard. 'Somebody may come prowling around the Palace whom you'd be *glad* for me to blow up.' And when they asked who such a person could be, she would never give a direct answer, but only shook her head, and began muttering about witches and dragons and other unpleasant creatures who – so she said – were still to be feared in this lonely part of the country.

*

When the children had finished their breakfast, the old lady drew them both towards her.

'Now listen,' she said, 'you two children are going many miles from home; you'll be all by yourselves, and you may have great adventures. That's just as it should be. Young people must learn to look after themselves, especially if they're royal.'

And out of her bag she drew a book, which she placed

on the table before them.

'That's my first present,' she said, 'and mind you don't lose it, or you'll have reason to be sorry.'

Jill picked up the book with an exclamation of delight. It was bound in white leather, with a border of seed pearls, and sewn on to the cover with tiny threads of white silk were three white peacock's feathers.

Jill opened the cover, and there, in letters of silver she read:

MRS JUDY'S ALPHABET OF MAGIC
BY
MRS JUDY

Underneath this title was the inscription:

'This book is dedicated to all children who want to be naughty, in the hope that it may help them to be naughty without being found out.'

The children stared at their grannie with great astonishment. Was it possible that any grown-up person could be so sensible, and have such excellent ideas? Evidently it *was* possible, for the old lady winked and nodded. 'Yes,' she chuckled, 'you'll find it all in that book. Not how to be *very* naughty, of course, but naughty enough. For instance, if you look up the letter P you'll find Peaches, and you'll learn exactly how to remove peaches from the wall without the gardeners ever finding out who took them. But we haven't time to look at the book now. Put it away and look at my other present.'

From her pocket she drew a little round box.

'But, Grannie, it's a compass . . .' began Jack, and then he stopped. He was going to tell her that they already had a compass, but he did not want to hurt her feelings.

'This is not an ordinary compass,' continued the old lady, as though she had guessed his thoughts. 'It is a magic compass! Come and look at it more closely.'

The children bent over the little round box. At first sight it looked like any other compass, except that it was obviously very old, and badly in need of a dusting. But as they peered through the glass, their eyes were puzzled.

'I can't see any of the usual signs,' said Jill.

'And which is North and which is South?' asked Jack.

'North and South!' retorted his grannie, in a tone of contempt. 'Why do you want to bother with things like North and South?'

'Well – to find out which way we are going, of course.'

'You talk almost as foolishly as a grown-up. They're always worrying about whether they're travelling to places where they'll be North or South, when all they *ought* to be thinking about is whether they're travelling to places where they'll be *happy*. That's something that no ordinary compass will tell you.'

'And will this one tell us?'

'At least it will tell you of places where you *won't* be happy. Can you read the four signs on it?'

They peered still closer. Gradually they spelt out the tiny letters . . .

'Where it should say North I can read D . . . A . . . N – DANGER!' whispered Jack.

'And where it should say East I can read B . . . E . . . W – BEWARE!' breathed Jill. 'I don't think it's a very nice compass,' she complained.

'Look at the other two signs,' ordered their grannie.

'H . . . A . . . P – HAPPINESS! That's to the West!' read Jack.

'And P . . . E . . . A – PEACE! That's to the South!' Jill nodded. 'I see the idea,' she said. 'But I still don't understand how . . .'

'Wait a minute,' interrupted the old lady. 'Watch this.'

Out of her pocket she drew a tiny bottle. 'This is deadly poison,' she said. 'I am going to put this by the side of the compass and you will see what happens.'

She placed it by the compass, and instantly the tiny needle swung round to the North, and quivered violently over the word DANGER.

'Oh, Grannie, how exciting!' cried Jill. 'Please – let me have the compass for a minute.'

'What do you want to do with it?'

'I want to take it to the window and point it towards the Mountain!'

'Very well.'

Together the children hurried to the window. Far, far away, through the towers and turrets of the Palace, they could just see the summit of the Mountain. It seemed to float in the sky like a silver cloud. They set down the compass and wached it in breathless silence. The compass was trembling more violently than ever. And it was pointing mid-way between the signs for DANGER and for HAPPINESS.

The old lady's face was very grim.

'Just as I thought,' she muttered.

Jill turned a pale face towards her. 'What does it mean?'

'It means, my dear, that you will both have to be very careful.'

'But careful of what?'

'I do not know. I am too old to tell the future any more.'

Jack put his hand in hers. 'We *will* be careful, Grannie. We really will.' He was terribly afraid that something might happen to stop their trip. 'And you won't tell Mummy, will you?'

The old lady shook her head. 'Certainly not.'

Which shows that she was really a very sensible old lady.

*

Goodbyes are always tedious, so we will not linger over them. We will not tell you how the children tiptoed into their father's bedroom, to receive his blessing and his good advice – which, like all the advice that fathers give to their children, was quite worthless and best forgotten. We will not tell you how many times their mother asked them if they had remembered to take their woolly vests, nor how often she warned them to be careful of talking to strangers. All children who set off on a holiday by themselves have had to go through these silly things, and know how tiresome they are.

In a few minutes we shall have finished with grown-ups. We have not time for them. Too many strange adventures

8

are awaiting us, out on the open roads, and far away, high up in the lonely mountains.

So let us come quickly to the last moment, outside the great porch of the Palace, with the children perched in the cart, and Moko, the donkey, tossing his head, and the Queen fluttering round to make sure that nothing had been forgotten.

Jill mounted the driving seat and took the reins in her hands.

'Goodbye, Mummy!'

'Goodbye, darlings!'

'Goodbye . . . goodbye!'

Moko started forward with such a jerk that the children almost fell from their seats. But a moment later he was trotting proudly through the great arch, over the draw-bridge where the sentries stood at the salute, down the long avenue of lime trees, and out on to the open road.

The adventure had begun.

2. Two Wicked People

The adventure had indeed begun, and in greater earnest than the children suspected.

For hardly had the dust from the donkey cart died down than two figures who had been hiding in the hedge opposite the Palace gates crept out on to the road, mounted their bicycles, and began to follow.

They had been hiding there since dawn, waiting for the children to come out. And we had better take a good look at them, for they are going to play a large part in our story.

Had you passed them on a summer day, bowling along on the open road, you would have thought that they were just a nice young couple going for a ride. You would never have guessed that one of them, who was called Sam, had murder in his heart, nor that the other, who was called Miss Smith, was in fact a witch. You would have had to look very closely to find anything unusual about them. And then, perhaps, you would have noticed that behind

Sam's short red beard, which he had grown as a disguise, his mouth was cruel and twisted, and that when he smiled, which was seldom, his teeth were sharp and pointed, like the teeth of a wolf.

As for Miss Smith, the witch – at first sight you would have said that she was as pretty as a picture. She was wearing a scarf of pale blue silk, which fluttered in the wind, and tangled itself in the wisps of her golden hair. But this hair was, in fact, a wig, for Miss Smith – who was three hundred and eighty-seven years old – had been as bald as a coot for over a century.

For a while these two wicked people pedalled along in silence, making no attempt to overtake the donkey cart, which kept at a distance of about half a mile ahead. Sam had a lot to think about, for this was the third time in his life that he had plotted against the children, and those of you who have read the other stories of their adventures* will remember that on the last occasion he was very nearly successful. But there was a great deal of difference between then and now. *Then* he had been thinking only of the ransom which he hoped to gain from their father after he had kidnapped them; *now* he was thinking only of his revenge, And when a man like Sam has revenge in his heart, there is nothing at which he will stop . . . not even murder.

He put his thoughts into words.

'This time,' he growled, 'there must be no mistake.'

'You've said that before,' snapped the witch.

'And I'll say it again. When I think of all the money I've paid you to get rid of those brats, I feel tired.'

'Not as tired as I do,' she retorted. Saying which, she dismounted and flung her bicycle on to the grass by the side of the hedge. 'I'm going to sit down.'

'What . . . already?'

'Why not?'

'We'll lose sight of the kids.'

* *The Tree that Sat Down* and *The Stream that Stood Still*, also in Lions.

'What's it matter? There's only one road, and we can easily catch them up.'

'Maybe we can. But when *you* sit down there's always trouble.'

Miss Smith shrugged her shoulders, as though she did not understand what he meant. But of course, she understood very well. For whenever she got off her bicycle to rest, and flung herself on the grass by the roadside, all sorts of the most disgusting creatures immediately crawled out of the bottom of the nearby hedges to welcome her, realizing that a friend had come among them.

So it was on this occasion. No sooner had she settled herself – choosing for a seat a large ants' nest – than there was a hissing and a rustling in the long grass, and in a few moments she was surrounded by an army of large black slugs, arching their backs and sticking out their horns, and bowing and scraping before her as though she was their Queen – as indeed she was.

'Look at the little sweety-pies!' she cried to Sam. 'Did you ever see anything so lovely and so slimy?'

'Don't you go putting those things near *me*,' growled Sam, edging away. 'It's not natural liking things like that.'

As he said this all the black slugs turned their horns towards him, and looked at him with a very hostile expression.

'There, you see, you've offended them, the poor little popsikins,' complained Miss Smith. 'You just haven't got a heart, that's what's the matter with you.' She turned again to the slugs. '*We* love each other, don't we, darlings?' All the slugs turned back to her and waved their horns. 'We understand each other, don't we?'

And she stretched out her hand, and very daintily picked up the largest, slimiest slug she could find, holding it close to her face as though it were a pretty little kitten or a nice little puppy.

'Isn't he beautiful? Isn't he the most slippery, slithery thing you ever saw?'

'Stop fooling and get down to business!' Sam barked.

'Isn't he the most slippery, slithery thing you ever saw?'

'How long d'you think it'll take you to get rid of those two brats?'

'Get *rid* of them? Really, what a crude thing to say!'

'Maybe it is, but you know very well what I mean. There's not room in this world for me and those kids. They've got to be finished with, and quickly.'

'That's easier said than done, unless you want to be had up for murder. We've got to be sure we don't leave any traces. And that means that I shall have to weave a lot of spells. And one thing I will *not* do is to be hurried when I'm weaving spells.'

'I don't see why we've got to have all this fuss and bother. Why can't we get it over at once? Why can't you just turn yourself into a snake one day, and creep up behind them and give them a nip?'

Miss Smith gave a contemptuous sniff. 'Really! The idea! What do you take me for?'

'I take you for a proper witch. At least, that's what I *did* take you for, though I'm beginning to doubt if you *are* a proper witch. You haven't turned yourself into anything for years.'

'Insulting!' she replied. 'That's what you are. And stupid, too. You talk as if it was as easy to change your body as to change your hat. It isn't. For one thing, it's extremely tiring. For another, things may go wrong.'

'Oh, you only say that because you can't turn yourself into a snake.'

The witch's eyes flashed with anger. She decided to teach Sam a lesson. She had no intention of turning herself completely into a snake, and she doubted if she could do so even if she tried. However, the first few steps are very simple – in fact, they are taught in the most elementary classes of every Witches' Academy for Young Ladies. So she closed her eyes and began to whisper Lesson One:

> Snake that hides in dirty ditch,
> Hear this cry, and help this witch!
> Snake that lurks in pool and pit,
> Gather near with spite and spit!

> Snake that slithers o'er the grave,
> Creep to me, my soul to save!

'Hey there!' cried Sam, drawing back in alarm. 'What's all that gibberish you're muttering?'

But she paid no heed. She could feel the spell beginning to work, and though she herself felt a little frightened, in case she should go too far, she could not draw back now. Creeping slowly towards him, stretching her neck and narrowing her eyes, she repeated the last lines of the spell:

> Now that I this song have sung
> Split my lips and fork my tongue!
> Kiss me with a poisoned kiss
> Till I hiss . . . and hiss . . . and hiss . . .

Pale as death she crept nearer, and as she did so a terrible hiss came from her, and out of her lips darted a tiny black tongue, flickering to left and right as though it were seeking something to sting. And to his horror Sam saw that the end of it was forked like a snake's.

'No! No!' Sam retreated from her, sweating and stumbling. 'That's enough! Stop it! That's enough, I tell you!'

The witch gave one long last hiss, and then she drew in her tongue. To tell the truth, she was only too glad to do so, because the whole thing had been most painful. She felt as if the end of her tongue had been almost bitten off, and there were all sorts of strange aches and shivers in her body, as though her bones had begun to melt and her skin to turn scaly. It only showed how careful you had to be with these old spells.

However, she was not going to let Sam see that she was upset.

Forcing a smile and pretending to be quite at her ease, she said: 'Well, I hope you're satisfied now.'

'You're not going any further?' enquired Sam, in a very shaky voice.

'Not if you behave yourself. But if you don't, there's no knowing what I might turn myself into, one of these days. It might be a snake or it might be a tiger. It might even be a crocodile.'

'All right,' he grunted. 'There's no need for us to quarrel about it. Only I wish you'd tell me what you mean to do.'

'That I certainly shan't.'

'I don't believe you know yourself.'

'Don't you? In that case you've got a big surprise coming to you, young man!' And with a fearful chortle the witch leapt on to her bicycle and began to pedal down the road so fast that Sam had difficulty in following her.

And so these two wicked people rode on through the day, scarcely speaking to one another, keeping their sharp eyes fixed on the children's cart some two miles ahead, which showed up like a little black spot on the Mountain road.

3. Caterpillar Calling

Dusk was falling before the children called a halt. Though they were still only on the lower slopes of the Mountain, they had climbed high enough to give them a wonderful view of the rolling hills and valleys. From far below came the muffled roar of the river, and over on the horizon they could see a faint glow of gold, which they rightly guessed must be shining from the lights of the Palace.

'We've come a long way from home,' whispered Jack.

Jill nodded. That was what she was thinking too. For a moment she felt homesick, and almost afraid, when she thought of how much further they had still to go.

'Look!' cried Jack suddenly. 'Aren't there two lights on the road below?'

'So there are.' Jill peered intently through the gathering darkness. 'Like bicycle lamps. Oh dear – I do hope nobody is following us.'

The children watched in silence.

'At any rate they don't seem to be coming any nearer,' said Jill.

'No. They've stopped still. All the same, there's something funny about them. A moment ago they were red, but now they're green . . .'

'And now they're yellow,' interrupted Jill.

'And now they've gone out altogether!'

They stared at each other in bewilderment. Then Jill forced a laugh. 'Anyway, they're nothing to do with us. Let's get the hamper out of the cart and start seeing about supper.'

If they had only known the meaning of those lamps – if they could have only seen Miss Smith, weaving her wicked spells by their light – they might not have felt so easy!

The children had planned to snatch a few hours' sleep after their supper, and then to get up again at midnight and travel on by the light of the moon. So as soon as they had finished, they said good night to Moko, who was browsing quietly by the side of a nearby stream, then laid out their mattresses underneath a cluster of giant pine trees, and curled themselves up in their rugs.

Soon Jack was fast asleep, breathing gently by her side. But though Jill shut her eyes as tightly as she could, sleep would not come to her. The day had been too exciting, too many strange things had happened – and for some reason which she could not explain, she felt vaguely uneasy. She seemed to hear whispers in the trees, and strange forms moving in the shadows. 'This is too silly,' she said to herself. 'I'm behaving like a baby. There's nobody here but Jack and me and Moko . . .'

Then suddenly she sat up with a start. This time there could be no doubt about it; she *had* heard something. It was a tiny cry, just behind her, very soft and high and squeaky, like the sound of a pencil on a slate.

She turned slowly round, holding her breath, wondering whatever it could be . . .

But she could see nothing. With trembling fingers she put out her hand for the compass which her grannie had given her before they set out on their journey. She lifted it close to her eyes and read it by the light of the moon. It was quivering, ever so slightly, between 'PEACE' and 'HAPPINESS'.

Jill gave a sigh of relief. So whatever it was that she might have heard, it could not have been a sound of danger. And then, just as she was about to lie down again, the tiny cry came once more. It was so close to her ear that she jumped back in alarm, and as she did so she saw that it came from a little woolly caterpillar that was sitting on the extreme top of a long blade of grass.

'Excuse me,' said the caterpillar.

'Was it *you*?' asked Jill in astonishment.

'I'm afraid so,' replied the caterpillar. And to Jill's dismay she saw two large tears drop from its eyes.

Jill leant forward, and tried to make her voice sound as soft and gentle as possible. 'Is anything the matter?'

'Everything's the matter,' replied the caterpillar.

'Would you like to tell me?' asked Jill.

The caterpillar took a deep breath, trying to summon up the courage to tell her his secret. Then out it came.

'I don't want to be a chrysalis,' he said.

Jill could hardly believe her ears. 'You don't want to be a *chrysalis*?'

The caterpillar shook his head. 'I just *won't* be a chrysalis. I'd rather die. In fact, I believe that if they ever made me be one, I *should* die.' As he spoke, two more tears formed in his eyes, and his whole body began to tremble, as though the thought of being a chrysalis was too dreadful to contemplate.

Jill looked grave, for she realized that this was a serious problem, and she had no idea how to meet it. She had read enough natural history to realize that every caterpillar must turn into a chrysalis, in order that later on he may turn into a butterfly. It was as natural for a caterpillar to do this as for a tadpole to grow into a frog or for a kitten to grow into a cat, and she did not see how it could possibly be prevented.

Besides, when one thought how nice it would be to turn into a butterfly, fluttering about among the flowers with brightly coloured wings, she could not see how any caterpillar would mind spending a short time as a chrysalis.

The caterpillar must have guessed her thoughts, for just as she was about to tell him what was passing through her mind, he spoke again.

'I know what you're going to tell me,' he squeaked. 'You're going to tell me that it would be lovely to turn into a butterfly.'

'Well,' confessed Jill, 'I *had* thought of something like that. Don't you think it would?'

'No. I think it would be perfectly horrible. I know I could never fly.'

'But if you had wings?'

'I shouldn't use them. I should fold them up and sit down all day on the grass. And *then* what would people say? But that's not the worst of it,' went on the caterpillar.

'It's being a chrysalis – that's the part I just couldn't stand. I should suffocate – I know I should.'

'But *other* caterpillars don't suffocate.'

'I can't help what other caterpillars don't do. I should suffocate.' His tiny voice rose to an even shriller squeak. 'How would *you* like to have to curl up inside a sort of bundle for weeks and weeks without daring even to move? How would *you* like to feel all sorts of horrid changes going on inside you without being able to stop them – all your legs falling off, and nasty great wings sprouting out of your back? And when it was all over, how would *you* like to come out as a quite different person, without knowing where to go or what to do? But you could *really* help me if you wanted.'

'How?'

The caterpillar turned his head, and his green eyes flashed in the direction of the cart, where Moko was grazing in the shadow of the trees. 'You could give me a lift,' he whispered.

'Up to the Mountain?'

'Yes. Up to the Mountain. Anything can happen up there.'

'But wouldn't you still have to be a chrysalis, even if you did go up to the Mountain?'

'No. I should get out of it somehow. I know I should. I should find some sort of magic which would stop me from ever growing up. *Please* give me a lift!'

'Oh, Jill, do let's give him a lift!'

Jill turned round sharply. It was Jack's voice.

'I thought you were asleep,' she said.

'I was, but I woke up, and I heard all he said. And I think it would be absolutely horrid to be a chrysalis.'

'Oh, do you? Do you indeed?' The caterpillar hopped off Jill's skirt and hobbled over quickly to Jack, who took him up and set him on his knee.

'Very well,' said Jill, 'he shall come with us. But first we really must get a little rest.'

'I know where he can sleep,' cried Jack. 'On the compass. It's just the place. He can curl up on it, and then there's no danger of our losing him.'

He held out his hand, and the caterpillar jumped into it. Then Jack took the compass, and put it by the side of the pillow, and the caterpillar hopped on to it, curled up, and blinked at them with his little green eyes.

'Are you comfy, Mr Caterpillar?' asked Jack, in a sleepy voice.

'Very comfy, thank you,' sighed the caterpillar.

'Then I'll say good night.'

'Good night.'

There were three long sighs, the rustling of blankets, and they were fast asleep. They went on sleeping, while the moon rose higher and higher, and the shadows danced across their faces. And then, another shadow fell across them, swooping nearer and nearer. But before we can tell you what it was, we must go back into the valley, and pay another visit to Sam and the witch.

4. A Very Bad Bird

While the children had been talking to the caterpillar, Sam and the witch were having their supper in a dark, lonely wood, some two miles below.

Miss Smith spread out a white sheet on the ground, and patted her hand on it as a sign that Sam should share it with her.

'No thanks,' growled Sam. 'I'm not sitting on *that*, thank you.' For he happened to know that the sheet had once been a shroud, and that Miss Smith had stolen it, years ago, when it was lying over the body of a most unpleasant murderer.

'Please yourself,' she retorted, shrugging her shoulders. 'At least let me offer you a sandwich.' And she held out a most tempting looking sandwich, wrapped in tissue paper.

Sam's eyes glittered. He was one of the greediest people

you could ever meet. All the same, he did not trust Miss Smith, nor her tastes.

'What's in it?' he demanded.

'Sliced slugs.'

'Sliced *what*?'

Miss Smith's mouth was rather full, and when she repeated her answer it sounded like 'Schliced schlugs'.

'Schliced *black* schlugs,' she added. 'Much nicer than the white ones.'

Sam drew back as though she had struck him.

'You mean to say you eat those things?'

'Why not? They're delicious. Fresh as a daisy too. I picked them in the hedge this afternoon, as a special treat.'

Sam shuddered. 'Don't you dare put 'em near *me*.' He retreated to a safe distance, sat down on the trunk of a fallen tree, and began to munch a cold sausage in gloomy silence.

'You're not very sociable,' sniffed the witch. 'After all, you're *supposed* to be my husband. And this is *supposed* to be our honeymoon. And you're *supposed* to be madly in love with me.'

For answer Sam gave a hollow laugh.

'All right . . . laugh away. But you'll have to laugh on the other side of your face when we're in company.'

'What sort of company?'

'All the animals we shall meet on the Mountain.'

'Why do we have to meet 'em at all?'

'Because we shall need their help. We've got to find somebody who'll put us wise to things . . . show us the lie of the land . . .'

Suddenly she paused, and put her fingers to her lips. 'Don't say anything for a moment,' she whispered. 'I believe something's going to happen. Pretend to be asleep.'

They stayed there, very still, two dark figures in the moonlight, lying down with half-closed eyes. Across their white faces darted the shadows from the moonlit clouds, but there was another shadow that came from no cloud but from the outstretched wings of a big black bird. It swooped over them once, twice, thrice, as though it were making sure that they were really asleep. Then, very gently, it fluttered down, perched on the back of the witch's bicycle, and began to peer at the carrier which was strapped behind.

As smoothly as a snake Miss Smith glided towards it. There was a flash of a white hand, a squawk of terror, and the jackdaw was struggling in her hands.

*

'Good evening!' crooned Miss Smith. 'This *is* a pleasant surprise.'

'Let me go . . . let me go!' squawked the jackdaw.

'But you can't leave us when we've only just met! That wouldn't be *polite*, would it?' And she gave the jackdaw's tail a vicious tug. 'Besides, you quite frightened my poor husband, didn't you?'

'That's right,' muttered Sam, wondering what all this was about.

'And when he gets frightened, he's apt to take out his gun and begin to shoot things. And you wouldn't like to be *shot*, would you? You wouldn't like to be shot dead, and fall to the earth, like a cold stone?'

She bent closer to the jackdaw, and her green eyes glittered like the eyes of a viper. And the light from her eyes seemed to mingle with the light from the eyes of the jackdaw, and in a strange way it was the *same* light; it blended; it was the light of wickedness.

They were kindred spirits.

'I am going to like this big black bird,' said the witch to herself. 'We shall be friends.'

And through the jackdaw's twisted brain flashed the thought that he, too, was going to like the strange creature who was holding him so fast. In her hands he felt at home. He ceased his struggling, his wings relaxed. They stared at each other, two pairs of green eyes, glittering in the moonlight.

Miss Smith opened her hands. 'Fly away,' she cackled, 'if you still want to.'

The jackdaw fluttered on to a dead branch, and shook

his head. 'I don't want to, any more.'

'I knew we'd understand each other,' replied the witch. 'But first . . . tell me why you look so sad.'

And indeed, the jackdaw looked almost too sad to be true.

'It's . . . it's . . . it's what they're saying about me, up there on the Mountain. That I'm a . . .' Once again he hesitated. Then out it came with a blurt '. . . that I'm a thief!'

'A thief!' Miss Smith's eyes sparkled. That was a welcome word, a pretty word, a word that made her feel nice and cosy. A thief! Yes, that was delightful. Her heart warmed to Mr Jackdaw.

She leant forward and smiled at him, very sweetly. 'And *are* you?'

'Certainly not!' he squawked. 'The idea!' He drew himself up, and ruffled his feathers, and breathed in and out very fast, as though such a suggestion were most insulting. But the witch noticed that his eyes did not meet hers. They shifted this way and that, as though he were lying. As, of course, he was.

'Are you sure?' She still smiled sweetly at him.

'Sure? Of course I'm sure.'

The witch sighed, ever so gently. 'That's a pity,' she said. 'Because I *am* a thief.'

The jackdaw could hardly believe his ears. 'You? A thief?'

'Certainly. A very good one too.'

The jackdaw was too bewildered to speak.

'To prove it,' continued the witch, 'you have only to turn round. While we have been talking I amused myself by removing three feathers from your tail. They are now sticking up on the handlebars of the bicycle, immediately behind you.'

His beak gaping with astonishment, the jackdaw slowly looked round. There, sure enough, were three of his own feathers, sticking up on the handlebars.

'I . . . I . . . I can't believe it,' he stammered, turning back again.

'It's all right,' laughed the witch. 'You needn't worry; I won't take any more. I just wanted to show you that when I say a thing, I mean it. And now, come here, and listen to what I have to say.'

The jackdaw hopped on to her knee, and blinked up into her face with his wicked green eyes. For a moment there was silence. The witch was thinking hard. Then suddenly she had an idea.

'You are in danger,' she croaked.

'Me?' The jackdaw blinked nervously. 'How? Who? Why?'

For answer the witch pointed a skinny finger up the hill-side. 'Two Humans. Sleeping up there. On their way to the top of the Mountain. They're after you.'

'Me? But why?'

'They want to catch you and put you in a zoo!'

The jackdaw began to tremble violently. For though he was only a bird, and though he lived far from the haunts of men, all wild animals tremble when they hear that word 'zoo'. To them it has the same sound as 'prison' has to us.

'Yes,' continued the witch, who had not failed to note the effect of her words, 'they want to catch you and clip your wings and shut you up in a cage, and show you to hundreds and hundreds of Humans who will push their fingers at you and prod you in the ribs till you are black and blue, for ever and ever and ever!'

'Oh no!' squawked the jackdaw. 'I couldn't bear it!'

'You'll *have* to bear it,' retorted the witch, 'unless you do as I say.'

'I'll do anything – absolutely anything!'

'Well, those two Humans up there have got a compass which means a great deal to them, because whenever they want to find anybody, all they have to do is to whisper that person's name to the compass, and immediately the needle points to where that person is. For instance, at this very moment they may be bending over it, whispering "Jackdaw, Jackdaw"! And the compass will be pointing straight down here!'

The poor jackdaw began to tremble even more violently

than before, and he cast a fearful eye up the hillside, as though he expected to see a horrible sort of finger pointing at him.

The witch patted him playfully on the head. 'It's all right,' she laughed. 'There's no danger for a little while; they're still asleep. But I want you to fly up, this very minute, fetch that compass, and bring it back to me.'

The jackdaw fluttered on to the branch of a tree that pointed to the open sky. Then he took a deep breath and stretched his wings.

'And mind you come back,' cried the witch. 'Otherwise . . .' and she drew her finger across her throat as an awful warning.

With a single swoop the jackdaw soared aloft.

*

'That's the last we'll hear of *him*,' growled Sam.

'I beg to differ,' snapped the witch.

'And anyway, what use have we got for a silly old compass in these parts?'

'You'll see, when the time comes.'

'If it ever *does* come.'

The witch made no answer beyond a haughty toss of her head. All the same, as the minutes ticked by, she began to grow anxious. She wondered if she had been rash in letting the jackdaw escape so easily; it might have been better to keep him for a few days, and tame him till he was completely in her power. However, it was too late to think of that now. Besides, she had a queer feeling that the jackdaw would *want* to return, of his own accord, that just because he was such a wicked bird he would fly back to her as though he were flying home.

And she was right. Ten minutes had barely passed before the black shadow fell over them once more. It was the jackdaw.

'What did I tell you?' cried the witch, leaping to her feet.

The bird skimmed through the branches and alighted breathlessly on the witch's shoulder. In his beak was a little round object that he dropped into her hand.

'The compass!' cried the witch, seizing it greedily. She turned to the jackdaw. 'You have done well, my friend. Nobody saw you?'

'No. The Humans were fast asleep,' panted the bird.

Miss Smith set the compass beneath the strange, flickering candlelight. Sam and the bird bent over her shoulder.

'Well, that's a rum-looking object, I must say,' growled Sam. 'It's quivering fit to bust, and it's pointing at us.'

'Yes. And do you see what it's saying?'

Sam bent closer and read the sign 'DANGER! BEWARE!' And now it was his turn to give a long, low whistle. 'So that's the idea!'

'That *was* the idea. But it won't be the idea much longer.'

With nimble fingers she flicked off the glass top. Then she took a tiny screwdriver, and unfastened the centre piece. It was now only a matter of seconds to twist the dial around and screw it up again.

'Now look what it's saying.'

He bent over it once more, and his mouth stretched into a cruel grin. 'PEACE! HAPPINESS!'

'Yes. And it's still pointing at us.'

Sam rubbed his hands together in glee. 'That's a corker!' he chuckled. 'That's a juicy one. That's the best idea we've had in years.'

'We?' retorted the witch. 'Did I hear you say *we*? I don't seem to remember that you had very much to do with it.'

'And it was I who had to steal the compass,' squawked the jackdaw, who was beginning to feel very huffy at being left out of things.

'So it was my dear,' said the witch, in a soothing voice. 'And very clever and quick you were about it, too. And now you've got to be just as clever and quick, and return it before they wake up. And when you come back I shall give you a special present.'

'What sort of present?' demanded the jackdaw, who was still somewhat offended.

'A beautiful sandwich of sliced black slugs!'

The jackdaw hopped up and down with excitement, and his eyes glistened greedily. And without any further ado he snatched the compass, tightened his beak firmly round it, and soared away through the moonlit branches.

'Well,' growled Sam, 'I must admit that you've earned your money tonight.'

The witch had every reason to be pleased with herself. She had done a good night's work. The magic compass, which had been the children's surest friend, had been changed, by a single twist of her wicked fingers, into their worst enemy. There was no end to the mischief which that little box might work.

She spoke her thoughts aloud. 'Yes,' she chuckled, 'I think we can say we've won the first round. He he! Ha ha! Ho ho!'

Her laugh was like the echo of the wind sweeping over a rainswept graveyard. But what she said was all too true.

5. An Eagle and an Imp

The dawn came bright and clear, and it was in high spirits that Jack and Jill, with their new friend the caterpillar, set out on the final stages of their journey. For how could they guess the deadly change which had been made in the compass which they trusted so completely? In high spirits, too, were Sam and the witch and the jackdaw, who were following at a discreet distance, keeping a sharp eye on their future victims.

But there was one person on the Mountain that morning whose spirits were by no means good. This was Mr Eagle, who might be described as the Lord of the Mountain – in the sense that he was the chief judge and law-giver, and that all the other creatures looked up to him and respected him.

From the very moment that he had opened his eyes on this particular morning, Mr Eagle had felt that something unpleasant was going to happen, but for the life of him he could not tell what it would be. He lay there in his warm nest, with his big beak resting on the edge, blinking in the sunlight, trying to think why he should have this strange feeling of unrest. From his lofty perch he could see for many miles around, and his eyes, which were as powerful as telescopes, could detect nothing wrong. All seemed quiet and in order.

And then, he suddenly turned his head to the left, and as he did so, he gave a little squawk of annoyance. For there, some two miles below, was a speck of vivid red. That red patch meant TROUBLE. For it came from the red flag which was kept in his office, and it had been hoisted by his old clerk, Mr Crow, as a sign that something very urgent, or even very dangerous, had happened, and that his presence was immediately required. Why on earth had Mr Crow hoisted that flag?

Well, there was only one thing to do; he must fly down and see for himself, and deal with the trouble, whatever the trouble might be.

He opened his wings, swayed for a moment from side to side, to test the current of the wind, and then, like a diver, he shot into space. Down . . . down . . . down he swooped, and as he descended, so the scene changed beneath him. The red flag came closer, closer, till his shadow fell across it. He wheeled sharply, and for a few seconds he hovered aloft, casting a stern eye over the rolling hills and vales, in case anything should have escaped his attention. He could see nothing amiss.

So much the worse for Mr Crow, he thought, if he had brought him all this way for nothing. Whereupon he glided through the narrow doorway, perched on his great desk, and struck the bell.

*

'Mr Crow! Mr Crow!' he cried. 'We are waiting!'

Through the door of the office hopped a very singular individual, an ancient crow, with rusty black feathers and very bent legs and a very long beak. Although Mr Eagle, in his heart of hearts, was really devoted to his old clerk, he often wished that he would smarten up his appearance, just a little. He felt that anybody so shabby must be bad for business. And yet in spite of Mr Crow's shabbiness there was something about him that seemed to command respect. Perhaps it was his old white collar, which hung round his neck like a broken soup plate. Or perhaps it was his spectacles, which he had snatched off a Human rubbish heap, years ago, when he had been a gay young crow, flying about on all sorts of harum-scarum adventures. The glasses had long disappeared from these spectacles; they were nothing but empty frames; but Mr Crow always pretended that he could not see a thing without them. Which was a very convenient idea, because if he was ever feeling lazy, or was faced by some problem which was beyond his understanding, he always pretended to have lost his spectacles.

'What is the meaning of this?' cried Mr Eagle, as soon as Mr Crow stood before him.

'It's Humans, Your Worship,' gulped Mr Crow.

'*What* did you say?' Mr Eagle had heard only too clearly what Mr Crow had said, but he needed a moment to recover from the shock.

'Humans,' he gulped again.

'How many Humans?' he demanded.

'Two, Your Worship. Or four.'

Mr Eagle frowned fiercely. 'What do you mean – two or four?'

'Well, Your Worship, four or two.'

'Are you trifling with me, Mr Crow?'

'No, sir.'

'Where *are* these two – or four – Humans?'

'I don't know, Your Worship.'

'I am beginning to lose my patience, Mr Crow. You get me down here, at the greatest possible inconvenience, and when I ask you why, all you can do is to babble about two – or four – Humans, whom you have not even seen.'

'I didn't say I'd seen them, Your Worship. It's the Imp who's seen them.'

'The Imp?' Mr Eagle suddenly sat up very straight on

32

his perch and opened his eyes very wide. 'Did you say the Imp?'

'Yes, Your Worship. Master Imp himself.'

'Then why in the name of goodness didn't you tell me so before?'

Mr Eagle now realized that this was indeed a crisis.

For the Imp of the Mountain was a very important person indeed. One might almost say that he *was* the Mountain, because it was only through this strange, shadowy creature that the Mountain ever made His wishes known; it was only the Imp who had the key to the Mountain's secret heart, only the Imp who could listen to those distant rumblings and tell the animals what they meant.

'When did the Imp tell you this?'

'Early this morning, Your Worship. And as soon as he told me I hoisted the red flag.'

'Quite correct, Mr Crow, quite correct. You could do no less. And where is the Imp now?'

'He's running to see you at this very moment, Your Worship.' Mr Crow turned round and stared through the open doorway. 'In fact . . . here he is!'

*

Into the room leapt a boy in green; he had a green hat and a green shirt and green trousers and bright green shoes. So swiftly did he flash into view that for a second you would have thought that his feet were not touching the ground. And so strange were his clothes that he looked more like a little green tree than a boy – a green tree swaying in the wind. Each time that he moved there seemed to be green shadows on his pale face, and green lights in his dancing eyes.

'Master Imp,' cried Mr Eagle, 'is this true?'

'About the Humans?' replied the boy. 'Yes, it's true all right.' And he burst into a peal of laughter, the strangest laughter you ever heard, cold and clear and sweet, like the laughter of a mountain stream as it tumbles over the rocks into the valley.

'Surely Master Imp, this is no time for laughter?'

'Why not? I think it's rather fun.' And he laughed once more.

Mr Eagle was bewildered. He had expected the Imp to be just as worried as he was himself; he had been prepared for him to say that they must call all the animals together, and form them into a great army, an army of claws and teeth and beaks and growls and snarls and spittings, and chase these wretched Humans away for ever. That would have been tiresome enough, and it would have meant a great deal of work and organization. However, at least it would have been something that he could understand.

But his laughter, he could not make it out. If the Imp had been one of the animals, he would have put on a terrible frown, and told him not to make a fool of himself. But as the Imp was the messenger of the Mountain, he had to be treated with respect. Mr Eagle turned again to the Imp.

'Does the Mountain know about the Humans?'

'Of course the Mountain knows. He knows everything. There isn't anything you can keep from *Him*.'

'And what does He say?'

'He doesn't say anything; He's lying low and saying nothing. He's waiting and seeing. That's what He's doing. Waiting. And seeing.'

Mr Eagle trembled slightly. Through the narrow porch he could see, far away in the distance, the tip of the crater of the Mountain, and for a moment it seemed to look like a huge, solitary eye, watching him from the clouds.

'What shall we *do*?' said the Eagle, after a long pause.

The Imp did not reply. He knew what Mr Eagle expected him to say. Chase them away! That was it. Send them back to where they belong! But he could not say it.

For to tell the truth, the Imp did not *want* the Humans to be chased away from the Mountain. He was glad – yes, glad – that they had come. He felt strangely excited that at last there was a chance of meeting people who looked like himself – people who stood upright on two legs, as he

34

did, instead of crawling about on all fours like the animals
– people with two arms, like his own, and a clear white
skin, instead of fur or feathers.

Of course, he could not tell Mr Eagle what he was
feeling; Mr Eagle would have been greatly shocked and
upset. Ever since the Imp had been a baby, right from the

Found him half naked and starving

earliest days when the animals had found him, half naked
and starving by the side of a lonely road on the hillside,
he had been taught to beware of Humans, to avoid them
at all costs, for they would only do him harm. And later,
when he began to grow up, and when, from time to time,
he had caught sight of a Human in the distance – far below

in the valley, or flashing on horseback across the skyline—
he had always been told to run away. 'If you follow them,
you will be lost,' they had warned him. 'But I look so like
them,' he had pleaded. 'Surely I must be Human too?'
Which made the animals very agitated indeed, and brought
forth a great roar of anger from the Mountain. He had
been told that it was wicked to say things like that, and
that if he ever said them again the animals would chase
him away, and that once more he would be naked and
alone. And since he loved the animals very much, he had
never spoken to them about it again.

But one day, when he had learned the secret of the
Mountain—when he climbed far into the Mountain's heart
and spoke to the Mountain Himself, as none of the animals
have ever done—he had asked the Mountain to tell him
what he really was.

'If I am not Human, what am I?' he had cried. 'Tell me,
Mountain! Tell me!'

He had asked that question as he stood on the edge of
the great crater—his arms flung wide, his little green body
outlined against the red glow that came from the flames
beneath. And out of the steam and the curling smoke had
come the Mountain's voice: 'You are the Imp . . . you are
my Imp . . . you are the Imp of the Mountain! And it is
through you that I shall give my commands!'

It was a proud little boy who had clambered back into
the fresh air after that great experience—a little boy with
a shining face and a heart beating high. When the animals
saw him coming towards them they knew that something
very wonderful had happened to him, and that from now
on he would be like a Prince among them.

Ever since then the Imp had accepted their trust, and
had tried to live up to it. But if they had only known, he
was still a little boy at heart—just a little boy, who was
longing to play!

*

So now you see why the Imp found it so difficult to answer
Mr Eagle's question.

'What shall we *do?*' repeated Mr Eagle, still more urgently.

There was another long pause. Then at last the Imp replied: 'I do not think that we should do anything until the Mountain has spoken.' That at least would give him time to think – even to get to know the Humans and make friends with them.

'Nothing at all?' demanded Mr Eagle, with some surprise. 'No bitings? No scratchings? No nippings? No stingings?'

'Certainly not any stingings!' replied the Imp.

'Not even any *peckings?*'

'Not a single peck. Particularly from you, Mr Eagle. When *you* peck, it's apt to be fatal.'

Mr Eagle modestly lowered his eyes. 'You flatter me, Master Imp. Very well, it shall be as you say.' He banged the bell. 'Mr Crow! Mr Crow!'

Through the door hopped the shabby black bird, looking more nervous than ever.

'Take down this notice, Mr Crow.'

'Yes, sir.'

TO ALL WHOM IT MAY CONCERN.

FOUR HUMANS HAVE ARRIVED ON THE
MOUNTAIN.

KEEP CALM!

THE SITUATION IS WELL IN HAND.

UNTIL FURTHER NOTICE THE FOLLOWING
ACTIONS AGAINST THE HUMANS ARE STRICTLY
FORBIDDEN: —

ALL

BITINGS

SCRATCHINGS

NIPPINGS

STINGINGS

PECKINGS.'

Here Mr Eagle paused, while Mr Crow feverishly scratched away with his old quill pen.

'I suppose we may show *some* disapproval, Master Imp?'

'Such as?'

'Well . . . an occasional growl, or even a hoot?'

The Imp shook his head. 'You'd better add that the following are also forbidden . . .

ALL GROANINGS AND GROWLINGS,
HOOTINGS AND HOWLINGS,
MEWINGS AND MUMBLINGS,
ROARINGS AND RUMBLINGS.

'I think that covers the lot,' he said. 'If you'll sign it. Mr Eagle, we'll hang it up on the door.'

'It's a great responsibility,' said Mr Eagle, taking up his pen. 'I only hope we are doing right.'

He scrawled his signature across the bottom of the page.

'And now,' said the Imp, 'I must be going.'

He swept Mr Eagle a low bow, straightened himself, turned, and darted from the room. If you had been standing outside that little hut, as he came out, you would have seen a flash of green, and heard a tinkle of laughter, and that would have been all. So swiftly did he move that he would have vanished before you could turn round.

6. Mountain Mystery

It was late afternoon before the children finally called a halt. And they halted, not because they were tired, but because they had found the absolutely perfect place to pitch their tent.

It was a small flat piece of land, rather more than half way up the Mountain. It was about the size of a tennis-court, and it looked as though it had been carved out of the hillside by a giant chisel. Above them the cliffs rose sharply to the clouds, with a stony path leading upwards through clumps of gorse and heather. On each side were thick pine-woods, through whose branches the wind sighed and sang, and they stood there, taking deep breaths of the clear, clean air.

But it was the stream which made them really decide that here at last was the place they were seeking. It tumbled down the cliffs like a shower of diamonds, and as they looked up they saw the sunbeams painting little rainbows in the spray. About a hundred feet above them it plunged into a hole in the rocks; then it came dancing out again, just by the edge of the pinewoods.

'It's just what we dreamed of,' whispered Jill. 'The cliffs will give us shelter, and the forest will give us firewood, and the stream will give us water . . . When we've got the things out of the cart, I'll go off and get some firewood and you can start putting up the tent.'

In a very few minutes they had unloaded the cart, in the shadow of the cliff where they planned to pitch the tent. Moko ambled off to the stream to have a drink of water, which he richly deserved.

'Well, that's that!' said Jill. 'And now I'm off to fetch the firewood.'

*

As soon as Jill had gone off to the pinewoods, Jack began to set up the tent. The first thing to do was to drive the pole into the ground. What fun it would be if he could drive it in, all by himself, and have it firmly fixed before his sister returned.

So he ran to the cart, chuckling with glee, and a moment later he was back again, dragging a pair of steps behind him with one hand, and clutching a big hammer in the other.

He prowled about, searching for a suitable piece of ground into which to drive the pole. In parts there was only hard rock; but here and there were patches of earth, which felt firm and solid when he stamped upon them. In a little while he had found the very place – a deep narrow seam of heavy clay, with rock on either side of it. The clay would be just the right sort of stuff to take the pole, and the rock round it would give an extra support.

So he set up the steps, went over and fetched the pole, and clambered slowly up, gradually pushing the pole into an upright position, till he was standing on the top rung.

Yes, the pole was quite straight, and its point was in just the right position on the little band of clay. He gripped the hammer tightly, and raised it above his head, aiming carefully, so that he should give the pole a big bang that would drive it well into the earth.

And now, something very extraordinary occurred. For as the hammer struck, driving the sharp point of the pole deep into the earth, there came, at the same time, a low muffled growl from far below. Jack looked around him, startled, wondering whatever it could be. It certainly wasn't an animal – at least, it was like no animal that *he* had ever heard. And it couldn't be thunder, because thunder came from above and not below. Nor could it be anything like an earthquake, for the ground was not moving. Perhaps he was imagining things. Anyway, this was no time for dreaming; he must get on with his work.

Again he raised the hammer, bringing it down so hard and so true that the pole was driven quite deep. And again, at exactly the same moment, there came the long, low growl that he had heard before. But this time it sounded louder, as though it were coming nearer . . . whatever 'it' might be. And it did not die away quite so swiftly, but gave several little minor growls before it died away into silence.

Jack stayed at the top of the steps, clutching the pole, and swaying slightly, for he was feeling just a little bit frightened. What *could* be the meaning of this strange sound? It obviously seemed to have something to do with his driving the pole into the earth, but what? For an instant he wondered if there was some extraordinary sort of animal beneath him, and if he were driving the pole on to the roof of its lair; but that couldn't possibly be the explanation. For one thing, it wasn't an animal, it was more like an angry old man; for another, it was much too far away.

Well, whatever it was, it wasn't going to stop him putting up the tent, particularly as one more really good bang was all that was needed to make the pole secure. So for the last time he lifted the hammer, and though his hand was trembling, brought it down, true and strong and dead on the top-centre of the pole.

And now, the roar that followed was so fierce and so close that it was as though the earth were opening beneath him, and Jack and the steps and the hammer all fell down in one big heap together. He stayed there, too frightened to feel his bruises, wondering if the earth were going to open beneath him.

'Jack, whatever's happened? Are you hurt?'

It was Jill bending over him. Never in his life had he been so glad to see anybody.

'I heard the most awful clap of thunder,' she went on, 'so I came running back.'

'It wasn't thunder,' he began, 'at least, it wasn't *ordinary* thunder.' And then he suddenly checked himself, because he felt that he would frighten Jill if he told her that those awful noises had only been the result of his driving the pole into the side of the Mountain.

'What else could it have been?' she demanded. But she did not wait for an answer, for she had noticed that his knee was bleeding. 'Oh, Jack . . . what a nasty cut! Stay here and I'll get a bandage.'

While she was fetching the bandage, Jack decided that he would keep his story to himself.

'However did you do it?'

'I was fixing the pole, and I fell off the steps.'

'Oh, Jack – you shouldn't have tried to do it all by yourself!'

'I wanted it to be a surprise.'

'It is. And a lovely surprise, too.' She turned round to admire it. 'Just in the right place.'

Even as she spoke, there was a low, faint growl from the far distance.

Jill paused, with the bandage in her hand.

'Did you hear that?'

'Yes. I heard it.'

'Thunder, I suppose.'

'Yes – thunder,' he fibbed.

'I shouldn't be surprised if were were going to have a storm.'

'Nor should I,' said Jack.

'Wouldn't that be exciting?'

'Frightfully.'

But in his heart of hearts he feared that it might be a storm which would be more exciting than either of them would wish.

*

An hour later, after a very welcome dinner of hard-boiled eggs and toffee and ginger beer, Jack was feeling very much better. The tent was firmly fixed, and a bright fire was blazing outside.

Now it happened that while Jack and Jill were having dinner, the Imp was scrambling up the last few feet of the slope, threading his way through the thicket of wild roses and tiptoeing step by step towards them. Had you been standing there, watching for him in the half-light, you might hardly have noticed him, with his green stockings, his green gloves, and his jacket of green leaves; you might well have thought that he was just one of the wild rose trees, that was being tossed by the rising wind.

One last step, and he was kneeling in the shadow of the tent, listening. For a moment there was silence; and then Jill spoke. And as he heard the voice of the Human girl the Imp trembled; a strange feeling came over him, half joy and half pain, for it was a sound that he had never heard before. And yet . . . and yet . . . surely he *had* heard it before, long, long ago? He could not remember; it was like trying to listen to an echo on the other side of the Mountain, that drifted away before you could catch its meaning.

But now he felt, more than ever, that he must be friends with these Humans; he knew, beyond any shadow of doubt, that he belonged with them much more than with the animals among whom all his life had been spent. So he tiptoed round to the front of the tent, threw open the flap, and boldly stepped inside.

*

'Hullo!' cried the Imp, in his high, thin voice.

'Good gracious!' It was Jill speaking, for though both children had turned round sharply as soon as the Imp pushed his head through the tent, Jack's mouth was still too full of toffee to speak. 'Whoever are you?'

'Well,' replied the Imp, 'if it comes to that, who are *you*?'

'My name is Jill and this is my brother Jack.'

'I see.' The Imp folded his arms and pretended to look very stern. 'I am the Imp of the Mountain,' he said.

Jack gulped down his last bit of toffee. 'Whatever's that?' he said.

The Imp stared at him in amazement. 'You mean to say you don't *know*?'

Jack shook his head. 'Never heard of it.'

'I'm not an "it",' retorted the Imp. 'I'm **a** "he".'

Both little boys began to look quite angry, so Jill gently interrupted them. 'I expect it's because we're rather new to these parts,' she said. 'We only arrived today.'

'Anybody can see *that*,' snorted the Imp, indignantly. 'And that's why I've come to find out what you were up to.'

'We're not up to anything. We're just having a holiday.'

'We'll see about that.' The Imp frowned at them as though he suspected that they were up to something very naughty indeed. 'I should be surprised if the Mountain lets you stay after all.'

'*Lets* us stay?' echoed Jill in dismay.

'*Lets* us stay?' snapped Jack, who was rapidly losing control of his temper. 'What's the Mountain got to do with whether we stay or not? Who *is* this old Mountain, anyway? I'd like to . . .'

But before he could finish this sentence there was a shrill cry from Jill. 'The tent . . . the tent . . . it's falling down!' Even as she gave the warning, the sides of the tent began to sway violently backwards and forwards, while the pole in the middle twisted and turned as though it were being spun by invisible hands. While all this was happening, from far, far below, deep down in the earth, came a long, low growl, like distant thunder . . . a frightening noise that reminded Jill of a huge lion shut up in a dark, damp cave.

Forgetful of the Imp, the two children clung together, holding each other tightly; their feet seemed frozen to the ground; they could not move. Then, little by little, the growling grew fainter, the swaying of the tent became less violent, and slowly, very slowly, the tent pole ceased to turn. Still they waited, and at last there was silence.

The Imp was standing there in the doorway. He was very pale and he was trembling, but he managed to give her a smile.

'Phew!' he said, wiping his forehead with a tiny green handkerchief. 'That was a narrow squeak! I've never known Him to get so angry before.'

'Him?'

'Yes. Him. The Mountain.'

Jill stepped forward quickly, and put out her hand.

'Please . . .' she whispered, 'don't let's quarrel any more.'

The Imp, for once in a way, was at a loss. He grinned sheepishly and stared at her hand. Then he peeled off his little green glove, and took Jill's hand in his. She had the strangest feeling as he did so, for though it was a human hand, there was something different about it . . . it made her think of cool green water, and green leaves, and growing branches, as though she were shaking hands with a tree instead of with a little boy, as though there were green blood in his veins instead of red. But she smiled back at him and beckoned Jack.

'Look, Jack – we are friends!'

The two boys shook hands.

'And now,' said Jill, 'will you please sit down and tell us what it all means?'

7. The Shadow of a Skeleton

While these strange adventures were befalling the children, Sam and the witch had not been idle. Nor had their new friend, the jackdaw.

The more she saw of the jackdaw, the more was Miss Smith inclined to like him, and to congratulate herself on having persuaded him to join their party. Whenever they mounted their bicycles, she called to him to perch on her handlebars, and as they cycled along, in the heat of the afternoon, she constantly leant forward and scratched his head.

'Isn't he the blackest, shiniest, naughtiest creature you ever saw?' she crooned, blowing him a kiss.

Sam pulled a face at her. 'Aw! You make me sick, you and that old bird!'

'Don't you speak unkindly to him, or you'll regret it,' snapped the witch. 'He's worth his weight in gold.'

'Then why can't he take us to some place where we can spend the night, before it grows dark?'

'That's just what I'm going to do,' squawked the black bird.

'There! What did I tell you?' cried the witch. She gave the jackdaw an extra scratch on the top of his head. 'And where is this beautiful place you are taking us to?' she enquired.

'About a mile further on. Between those two cliffs up there.' He pointed with his beak in the direction they must follow. 'It's a cave.'

'A cave!' the witch gave an exclamation of delight. 'Now isn't that just wonderful! If there's one place I've always wanted to live, it's in a nice, big, dark, damp cave!'

'Damp?' echoed Sam, scowling at the jackdaw. '*Is* it damp?'

The jackdaw shook his head. 'Not enough to worry about.'

'Never mind,' sighed the witch. 'One can't have everything.'

'There's only one thing against it,' ventured the jackdaw.

'I believe I know what you're going to say,' suggested the witch. 'You're going to say that it's full of bats!' And before he could reply she went on, 'Well, I shan't mind that in the very least! To tell the truth, I *adore* bats. In fact, if there aren't any bats in it already, I shall probably get some, and hang them up on the roof, just to make me feel at home.'

'There aren't any bats,' said the jackdaw.

'Then what *is* the matter with it?' demanded Sam.

The jackdaw hesitated for a moment. Then he said: 'There's somebody in it already.'

'Well, what of it? I'll chuck him out.'

'I don't think you could.'

'What . . . me? Not chuck him out?' Sam blew out his chest. 'I could chuck anybody out! I'd knock the life out of him!'

'But there isn't any life in him to knock out. You see, he happens to be dead.'

As Sam staggered back, pale and bewildered, a shrill peal of laughter came from the witch.

'He-he! Ho-ho! That's a good one! *That* made you look silly, my precious Sam! Knocking the life out of a corpse!'

'He isn't a corpse,' corrected the jackdaw. 'He's a skeleton.'

'Ha-ha! Ho-ho! He-he! That's better still!' She pointed a crooked finger at Sam. 'Look at him! He's gone quite pale!'

'I'm not afraid of any skeleton,' snarled Sam.

The witch was so delighted by the prospect of meeting such a charming creature, and moving into such a desirable home, that she could delay no longer, and she leapt once more upon her bicycle, and began to pedal rapidly up the long, winding road, with the jackdaw flapping his wings on the handlebars, uttering little squawks of encouragement.

'A nice business I've let myself in for!' Sam muttered to himself, as he pedalled up the lonely track. As the sun sank, so his spirits sank with it. But they were to sink lower yet.

*

The crisis came about two hours later, when they had actually moved in. Apart from the skeleton, the cave was not as bad as Sam had feared; it was tall and roomy, there was not much damp, and apart from one or two stalactites hanging from the ceiling, which could easily be knocked off in the morning, it looked as though it could be made very comfortable.

But the skeleton, quite frankly, made him shudder. It stood propped up against the wall, and as the shadows from the fire flickered over its bones, it seemed as if the limbs were twitching, and the bare skull grinning in his direction. He would not know a moment's peace until he had got rid of it. So as soon as the jackdaw had gone to sleep in one corner, and Miss Smith had settled herself down in another, he tiptoed over towards it, with the idea of dragging it quietly outside, and tipping it over the edge of the cliff.

He had reckoned without the witch. For just as he was about to seize the skeleton, she opened her eyes, grasped

The witch was delighted by the prospect of meeting such a charming creature

what was happening, and leapt to her feet with a howl of anger.

'Don't you dare!' she cried, springing in front of the skeleton, and holding out her arms to protect it.

She looked so fierce that Sam stepped quickly back, and stayed there, gaping at her.

'Don't you dare!' she repeated, in a voice that trembled with wrath.

'I've had enough of this!' snarled Sam, stepping forward. 'I'm going to throw that darned thing over the cliff.'

'Keep back!' she hissed. 'I warn you for the last time — if you get up to any tricks . . .' She did not finish the sentence, but shook her finger at him with such a threatening expression that Sam realized there was nothing for him to do but give in. And so, cursing under his breath, he turned away, and began to make his bed.

*

On the following day Sam was woken by a most unpleasant smell. For a moment he could not think what it was, and then, as he rubbed his eyes and looked about him, he saw that it was caused by the witch who was brewing what she called her early morning coffee. It was hardly surprising that this 'coffee' should smell nasty to ordinary persons, for it was composed of a mixture of equal parts of dead nettles, dried toadstools and the wings of small but very disagreeable bats.

Wrinkling his nose in disgust, Sam pulled on his shirt and went outside to eat a sandwich. As he stepped through the mouth of the cave he took a deep breath of the clear, thin air, and stared about him. It was a glorious morning; high above the sun shone silver on the mountain-tops, and all the hills and valleys were bathed in silver light.

As he munched his breakfast he took out the pocket telescope he always carried about with him, and trained it in the direction of the children's tent, which, as we have already learned, was pitched on a little flat piece of land which jutted out from the Mountain higher up, at a distance of about a mile. As the tent came into view, Sam's mouth took on an ugly twist, for he could see the children playing outside it, and the very sight of them aroused feelings of murder in his heart. And then a puzzled look came into his eyes, for a third figure danced into the picture – the figure of a little boy in green, at whom they smiled and with whom they joined hands. Who on earth was this? Could it be a brother, or some friend they had brought along with them? But no . . . he knew that they had no brother, and if it had been a friend, he would have shown himself before. Sam frowned darkly. Whoever this newcomer might be, he'd better be careful, or he would be destroyed with the rest of them!

He switched the telescope from the tent, and pointed it down the valley, letting it wander idly from side to side. And then, all of a sudden, he held it rigid, and stared very hard indeed. The telescope had alighted on the most unexpected object. For a few moments he could not make out what it was; it might have been the skeleton of some gigantic animal, or it might even have been a vast rubbish heap. He stared even more intently, and at last it was clear to him. He was staring at the wreck of an aeroplane.

Sam gave a long, low whistle. This was interesting. This was something which might come in very handy in the future. Exactly *how* it would come in handy he did not know. But through his cunning little brain flickered all sorts of evil ideas, of which we shall learn more before long.

His thoughts were interrupted by the witch.

'A beautiful morning!' she said, taking a seat beside him. 'Delicious morning! Delicious coffee! Delicious everything! This morning I'm going to pay a call on our friends.'

'Friends? D'you mean those brats?'

'Really, my dear, how can you speak so disrespectfully of their Royal Highnesses?'

'Stop fooling, and tell me what you are going to do.' He leant forward eagerly. 'Are you going to poison them? Are you going to cast a spell over them?'

The witch cast him a look of disdain. 'Upon my word,' she sniffed, 'I seem to be talking to a barbarian. Poisons and spells indeed! At this time of the morning!'

'Well, what am I paying you for?'

Her eyes narrowed. 'You're paying me to get rid of them,' she hissed, 'and I *shall* get rid of them. But I shall do it in my own time.'

'Why not now? Why not this very minute?'

'For one very good reason.' She paused, and arched her neck and winked. As she did so Sam thought that never before had he seen anything so like a snake.

'And that reason is . . . that first I want some fun. And if I'm not mistaken, so do you!'

Sam nodded. She'd got something there. He *did* 'want some fun'. Now that they'd come so far, and waited so long, it would be almost a pity if they finished the business straight off. Better to lure them on, to play with them, to make friends with them, and then . . . to strike! But how?

The witch answered his question before he had time to put it.

'I'm going to tell them about the Treasure Trove.'

Sam blinked. 'What Treasure Trove?'

'Our own special Treasure Trove.'

'It's the first time I've heard of it.'

'It's the first time anybody's heard of it. Except, of course, Mr Jackdaw, who really put the idea into my head. Bless his heart!' And she turned to scratch the head of the big, wicked bird, who had just fluttered out from the cave to perch on her shoulder.

Sam was bewildered. 'Where *is* this Treasure Trove?'

The witch gave him another pitying look, such as you would give to a small and stupid child. Then she tapped her forehead. 'There!' she replied. 'That's where it is.'

Sam continued to gape at her. 'Are you crazy?'

'No. But I shall be if you're so dense.' She leant forward and explained, in a hard, cold voice. 'We are going to *pretend* that there is a Treasure Trove up here in the Mountain. We are going to pretend that it is full of gold and diamonds and rubies and emeralds!'

'But why . . . *why*? That's what beats me.'

'Because, you big, boring, beautiful idiot . . . it's the

very thing we want to give us the sort of fun we need!
We can fill their hearts with hope, and then we can break
them. But we can break more than their hearts; we can
break their necks! We can send them climbing up steep
cliffs, and then we cut the ropes and send them spinning
down on to the rocks below! We can . . .'

'Wait!' Sam sprang to his feet in excitement. 'I know
something we can do that's even better than that.' He drew
out his telescope and handed it to the witch, pointing it
down into the valley.

'The wreck of an aeroplane!' she exclaimed, peering
eagerly through the glass. Then she turned back to Sam,
with a bewildered expression. 'But I don't see how that
can be of any use to us.'

'I could rebuild it,' he chortled. 'Not the engine, of
course, but there's more than enough of it left to make a
glider. I did more difficult jobs than that in the war. And
this *is* war – *our* war!'

The witch was still puzzled. 'For the life of me, I can't
see the connection between the glider and the Treasure
Trove.'

'Oh – don't be so dumb,' he retorted. 'Why, you said it
yourself, only a moment ago. Didn't you talk about getting
'em to climb steep cliffs, and then cutting the ropes and
sending 'em hurtling down on to the rocks? Well, that's
good enough. But with a glider it'd be far better.'

'Go on,' whispered the witch, who was beginning to get
the idea.

'When you go up to tell 'em about this Treasure Trove
of yours, all you have to do is to say that it's in a very
difficult place – somewhere that can only be reached by
gliding down to it. There are dozens of places like that, up
in the mountains. And then, all you have to do is to add –
in an offhand sort of way – that we're building a glider to
get to it. Can't you see? Why, there isn't a kid in the
world who could resist the idea of hunting for a Treasure
Trove, and there isn't a kid in the world who could resist
the idea of flying in a glider. And once we've got 'em
in . . .'

The witch clapped her hands in delight. 'I get it!' she cried. 'Oh, it's a beautiful plan! It's divine! It's scrumptious!'

And so, a few minutes later, in a brand new dress of pink satin, with a smart pink hat and a pair of very pink high-heeled shoes, she was picking her way up the stony path to pay a call on the children, and to put into practice the first stage of her plan for their destruction.

8. A Witch on the Warpath

'Oh, dear!' cried Jill, in a voice of dismay. 'There's some-body coming to call.'

Jack threw aside the ball with which he had been play-ing, and ran to the edge of the cliff.

'So there is. Whoever could it be?'

Jill kept her eyes on the figure climbing up towards them. The witch was still too far away to tell whether she was somebody very nice or somebody very nasty, though she was certainly somebody very pink. And yet, for some reason or other, Jill's heart was heavy. She seemed to smell danger.

Danger! The word reminded her of the magic compass. How silly she had been not to think of it before! Why, this was just one of those occasions which Grannie had been thinking about when she gave it to them. She would put it to the test this very minute.

However, she did not wish to cause any alarm, and so she told Jack that she was just going to run back into the tent to tidy her hair, and asked him if he would receive the visitor, whomever she might be, in her absence.

The compass was lying by her pillow, and Jill picked it up and set it in the entrance to the tent, so that it pointed to the path up which the witch was climbing. No sooner had she put it there than it began to tremble more violently than she had ever seen before.

Fearing the worst, Jill bent over it.

It was pointing to the word . . . PEACE!

She gave a sigh of relief, and even as she did so she heard the witch's voice outside. A very pretty voice it sounded, for Miss Smith was a good actress; she could have given a perfect imitation of the cooing of a dove, if so required.

Jill was just about to put the compass away, when she noticed that it was trembling more than ever, so fiercely, indeed, that she feared the tiny needle might swing off its hinges. She frowned. Surely there was something odd about all this? Why should the needle be so agitated when it was pointing to PEACE?

To make a final test, she lifted it up, gave it a sharp tap, and set it on the ground once more, pointing in the opposite direction. And again the needle swung sharply round to Miss Smith, who was now only a few yards away. It stayed there, trembling as though it were trying to escape from its little case. And this time it gave the message . . . HAPPINESS!

Jill smiled to herself; what a silly she had been! The message could not be more clear. Whoever it might be outside, she was obviously a friend.

She put away the compass, pushed back the flap of the tent, and stepped out to greet Miss Peace and Happiness . . . in pink.

*

Miss Smith was at the top of her form. She had won Jack's heart by guessing his age as twelve, when she knew that he was only eight.

But what about Jill?

The witch decided to play her cards boldly. As soon as Jill walked out of the tent, she sprang to her feet, stepped forward, and swept a low curtsey. And then, before Jill could check her, she stood upright again, and pretended to be very confused and gave a little giggle, and stammered . . . 'Oh, please forgive me, Your Royal . . . I mean . . . oh dear, what *am* I saying? I know you don't want that sort of thing on your holiday, but I just couldn't help it. But I *promise* not to do it again!'

And as she stood there, clasping her hands, with her big eyes glittering in the sunlight – as they had glittered for no less than three hundred and eighty-seven years – she looked so pretty and appealing that Jill, too, found her heart melting. Particularly as the witch, after a few minutes, glanced at her watch and said, 'I really must be getting back to my husband. He has a bad cold and I don't like leaving him alone.'

It seemed to Jill very touching that anybody so pretty – and so pink – should be anxious to get back to her husband when she might have stayed out enjoying herself.

'Besides,' added the witch, 'he will be needing me to help him in his work.'

'And what is his work?' enquired Jill.

'As a matter of fact,' returned the witch, 'he's a wizard.'

*

She spoke quite casually, as though it were the most natural thing in the world for one's husband to be a wizard. However, the effect on her hearers was electrical.

'A wizard – a wizard! Oh, isn't that wonderful!' Jack began to jump up and down in sheer excitement.

Jill was not so sure if she liked the idea. Of course, she knew that wizards were not like witches – in fact, in many ways they were the opposite of witches. But somehow the thought of having a wizard on the Mountain made her feel vaguely uneasy.

'A *real* wizard?' she asked, gazing at Miss Smith with puzzled eyes.

The witch tossed her head in pretended indignation. 'Of

course he's a real wizard.'

'Of course he is!' echoed Jack reproachfully. 'Oh Jill, how can you ask such questions?'

'I'm so sorry,' faltered Jill, 'but you see, I don't know very much about wizards.'

'That's quite obvious,' retorted Miss Smith. 'I shouldn't be surprised if you were to tell me that wizards were something like witches!'

'Oh Jill!' cried Jack, 'you couldn't think such a thing!'

'No, of course not.' But the tone of Jill's voice was still uncertain.

'Well, let me tell you this,' lied Miss Smith, warming to her task, 'that if there's one thing my husband can't abide, it's a witch. I shouldn't be surprised if he was working himself up into a rage about some witch or other at this very moment.'

All this, as Miss Smith had intended, was just what Jill had wanted to hear. If Miss Smith's husband really hated witches as much as all that, he must obviously have all the right ideas.

So she sighed with relief, and smiled at Miss Smith, and held out her hand to make friends.

'Forgive me,' she said. 'It was just that I didn't understand.'

'Don't mention it,' replied the witch, and the two shook hands.

'Does he weave the most wonderful spells?' demanded Jack, when they were all friends again.

The witch hesitated; she was not quite sure how she ought to answer that question. She did not want to let the children think that Sam was a *very* powerful wizard; that would have spoilt all her plans. She had all sorts of wicked plots up her sleeve, which she would soon be putting into practice, and it was important that they should not suspect either her or Sam of any part in them.

So she said: 'Well, of course, he's very delicate, so he doesn't do as much as he used to.'

Jack's face fell. 'Oh dear! D'you mean he doesn't weave any spells at all?'

She had made a conquest of all of them

He looked so disappointed that the witch saw that she had made a mistake. At all costs she must keep the children interested; otherwise they might slip out of her clutches.

She quickly corrected herself. 'No, I didn't mean *that*,' she said. 'I only meant that he only weaves the *nicest* spells.'

'Do you think he'd teach any spells to me?' asked Jack eagerly.

'I'm sure he'd be delighted.'

'Oh, please say when! Could it be tomorrow?'

'I don't think it could be tomorrow. He has a little business to do first.'

'Will it take him very long?'

'I don't expect so. It's just a matter of finding a Treasure Trove. And one never knows, does one, with Treasure Troves?' She spoke very lightly, as though a Treasure Trove could hardly be regarded as of any interest, and even as she spoke she rose, and held out her hand to Jill to say goodbye. 'So charming it's been,' she murmured. 'Delightful, I'm sure.'

*

But Jill was so thrilled by the news of the Treasure Trove that she did not even see the witch's outstretched hand.

'Did you say a Treasure Trove?' she breathed.

'Yes. So silly of me, chattering about my affairs. I mustn't keep you a moment longer.'

But Jack was equally excited by the news. 'Is it very big?'

'Big?' The witch was drawing on her gloves. 'The Treasure Trove? Oh yes. It's huge. Quite enormous. What a very pretty view you have up here!'

'How enormous is it?'

She shrugged her shoulders. 'I suppose it would fill half the Mountain.' And then, to show that the matter was of no further interest . . . 'Quite the prettiest view I've ever seen. May I bring my husband to see it some time?'

'Fill half the Mountain!' echoed Jill, who had scarcely heard her question. 'Why, it must be the hugest Treasure

Trove in the world! Are there any jewels in it?'

'Pardon?' The witch was still pretending to admire the view.

'Are there any jewels in it?'

'Jewels?' The witch appeared to have forgotten what they had been talking about. Then she gave an affected little laugh. 'Oh, I see. You're still thinking of that old Treasure Trove! Jewels? Let me see. Well, there are rubies, of course.'

'Are there many rubies?' Jack's voice was breathless with excitement.

'About a million, so I'm told.'

'A million.'

'Yes. I'm afraid there are only a million. The reason there aren't any more is because they're all so huge. The smallest is the size of an egg.' The witch wrinkled her nose in assumed disgust. 'Vulgar, I call it. I should feel quite weighed down, wearing things like that. Still, my husband insists on finding them.'

'What will he do with them when he finds them?'

'He'll give them away. He always does.'

'Would he give one to me?' asked Jack.

'Of course. Dozens, if you like.'

How long the witch might have stayed there, telling them of all the wonders of the Treasure Trove, we shall never know, for at that moment the conversation was suddenly interrupted.

There was a flash of green, a tinkling laugh, and a voice behind her said: 'How do you do?'

*

Miss Smith turned sharply, and when she saw the little boy standing there in his green jacket and his green stockings and his green gloves, it was as much as she could do to stifle a scream, for her witch's instinct told her that she was in the presence of an enemy, who might do her a great deal of harm, although he was so small.

However, she controlled herself, sniffed back the puffs of green smoke which were trying to escape from her nostrils, forced a smile, and held out her hand.

'How d'you do?'

'I am the Imp of the Mountain,' said the little boy.

'Of course,' she replied, as though she had known it all along, although she could not possibly imagine who or what the Imp of the Mountain might be.

As though to answer her unspoken question Jack chimed in: 'He's very important, aren't you, Master Imp?'

A faint flush lit the Imp's cheeks. He smiled and shook his head.

'Oh, yes you are. You've got the key to the Mountain's heart.'

Miss Smith pricked up her ears. She was still completely mystified, but it was obvious that the Imp was a power to be reckoned with. So she continued to stretch her lips into the sweetest of smiles, though the effort was almost unbearable, in view of the large quantities of green smoke that were simply bursting to come out.

'Fancy that!' she exclaimed. 'That's a great honour, to have the key to the Mountain's heart.' Her sharp eyes wandered over him, as though seeking to find out if he had the key on him now.

'I don't carry it about with me,' returned the Imp.

Jill suddenly gave a cry of excitement. 'Oh, Master Imp, perhaps the Treasure Trove is right inside the Mountain! And perhaps we shall need your key to get it!'

'Treasure Trove?' The Imp gave her a blank stare. 'What's this about a Treasure Trove?'

All eyes turned on the witch.

It was a very awkward moment. She had to do some quick thinking. She guessed that the Imp would not approve of the Treasure Trove – that he might even guess that the whole plan was a fraud, and try to persuade the children to have nothing to do with it. And though she felt that if it really came to a battle of wits she could beat the Imp without much difficulty, she was not ready for him yet. So she began to talk very fast and vaguely, with the idea of distracting his attention.

'Oh, that old Treasure Trove!' she cried with a gay laugh.

'It's just a little idea of my husband's – nothing to speak of – just a few rubies – emeralds – oddments of all sorts – bits and pieces – gold . . .'

'Where is it?' interrupted the Imp.

'Ah – that would be telling!' And she laughed even more gaily, and turned round to the children and gave them a meaning wink. Which was very clever of her, for it seemed to bind them to her in a secret from which the Imp was shut out.

And that was what he felt, in his lonely little heart – shut out, all of a sudden. And that was why he had this feeling of resentment against this strange Human who had so unexpectedly walked into his life. An hour ago, he and the children had been like brothers and sisters. But now, this other Human – (for how could he guess that Miss Smith was a witch?) – had come between them, and everything was spoiled. And they would all go off and hunt for a treasure together, and they would not even ask him to go with them.

If he had not been a brave little boy he would have begun to cry.

'Dear me! I must be going.' The witch turned round and blew them all a kiss. 'We shall meet again!' she cried. Heavens! A tiny puff of smoke was beginning to sizzle out of her left nostril. She seized a handkerchief and stopped it up. And so, with a great deal of laughter, wavings of handkerchieves, stuffings of nostrils, winks and gulpings and blowing kisses, she hurried up the path, while they stood and waved after her.

For a moment after she had gone there was silence.

Then Jack said: 'I think she's a *lovely* lady.' He turned to the Imp. 'Don't you?'

The Imp hesitated. 'I . . . I don't know much about Humans. But tell me about the Treasure Trove,' asked the Imp eagerly, for he was longing to share in the great adventure.

'Well,' Jill began. And then she suddenly started. 'Whatever was that?'

A sharp explosion had interrupted her. They all turned

to see what had caused it. To their astonishment they saw a thick cloud of green smoke drifting out from behind a bush some way up the path. It curled and hovered and drifted, and then faded away.

The Imp's eyes were puzzled – more than puzzled – they were afraid. But he forced a smile and shrugged his shoulders.

'Oh, it's nothing,' he laughed. 'Just the Mountain – in one of His moods.'

And it is to the Mountain – and His moods – that we must now give our attention.

9. Doorway to Magic

As soon as the witch was safely out of the way, and had dwindled to a tiny pink spot climbing up the Mountain side, the Imp turned to the children and said: 'I'm glad she's gone, because I have a secret for you. I'm going to show you something nobody has ever seen before. It's a *terrible* secret!'

'Oh dear,' said Jill, 'if it's as terrible as all that, do you think we ought to see it?'

Jack jumped up and down with impatience. 'Please, Jill, please! We *must* see it!'

'But supposing the Mountain were to mind?'

'It's quite all right,' interrupted the Imp. 'I've asked Him, and He says He won't mind, not for this once, on account of your being royal. But if I were to show the secret to anybody who . . .' He did not finish the sentence, but shook his head gravely, as though the very thought of such a thing were too terrible to contemplate.

'Now then . . . follow me!'

He turned and led the way up the stony path, which curled and twisted within a few feet of the edge of the

cliff. As they climbed higher and higher, the view of the
valley below became more wonderful, with all the fields
looking like tiny squares of green silk, and all the streams
threading their way through them like threads of silver;
but Jill did not trust herself to look too often over the edge,
for fear she should grow giddy. Still they climbed, and
she was just going to ask the Imp if they might not call a
halt and rest for a moment, when he stopped in front of
them and turned round, with a grin on his face.

'Well, we're here! This is the front door.'

*

The Imp entered and the children followed. They were in
a long, winding tunnel, very low and very dark, and they
had to bend their heads so that they should not bump
them against the rocky ceiling. Jill felt Jack's fingers twine
more closely round her hand, and she guessed that he was
feeling frightened, as well he might be, for this was surely
one of the strangest places in the world. As they stumbled
on, round dark corners and over sharp rocks, she began
to wonder wherever they were going, and if they would
ever get out again.

And then, all of a sudden, the tunnel became wider, the
ceiling lifted, and they found themselves in a lofty hall.
All round the hall were little caves, and over each cave, in
bright red letters, was painted the word 'Private'. But some
caves were evidently much more private than others; and
Jill was quite puzzled by all the sorts of 'Private' that were
written up. There was . . .

VERY PRIVATE

and there was . . .

VERY VERY PRIVATE

and there was . . .

VERY VERY PRIVATE INDEED

and there was . . .

MOST EXTRA PRIVATEST

MOST SUPER-EXTRA PRIVATEST

MOST EXTRA-SPECIALLY-DREADFULLY PRIVATEST

MUCH THE PRIVATEST CAVE IN THIS ROOM
MUCH THE VERY EXTRA PRIVATEST CAVE IN THE WHOLE
MOUNTAIN. . .

And then, at the end of the hall:

BY FAR THE MOST AWFULLY EXTRA EXTRA PRIVATEST CAVE
IN THE ENTIRE WORLD

The Imp pointed to this last cave. 'That's the one we want,' he said. 'By the way,' he added, 'I think I ought to warn you that it's *private*.' Which seemed to Jill, in the circumstances, a rather unnecessary remark.

They tiptoed over to the cave.

'Climb up on this ledge,' said the Imp. 'Look out! It's rather slippery. I think I'd better go first and give you a hand.'

He took one leap and seemed to glide up the face of the rock; as Jill watched him she was reminded of a grasshopper or a little green lizard, so smoothly and swiftly did he move.

'Me next!' cried Jack, and somehow or other he scrambled up, though not nearly as easily as the Imp. Jill came last, holding on to the hands of both the boys.

'Now I want you both to stay quite still for a minute, and just *listen*. Not a word, mind you, and try not to breathe too hard.'

Both children stayed as still as mice, and Jack held his breath till he felt he would burst.

'Can't you hear anything?'

They shook their heads.

'That's the worst of being Human,' said the Imp, in a superior tone of voice. 'All Humans are half deaf.'

Jill looked rather annoyed by this statement. 'We're not deaf at all,' she protested. 'It's just that there isn't anything to listen to.'

'Then come closer. Right up against the rock.'

They scrambled towards him till their faces were almost

touching the rock's face.

'That's better. Now bend down till your ear's *touching* the rock.'

'Oh!' Jack gave a sudden giggle. 'It feels cold.'

'Ssh! Listen!'

Silence. And then, through the rock, the children heard it . . . the sound of a stream, faint but clear, rushing through the dark secret caves above them. Though it was so far away, the sound came quite distinctly, gurgling and laughing, as though the swift waters were chattering together as they hurried along.

'Hear it?'

They nodded, but said nothing.

'Well, you needn't look as though you'd seen a ghost,' scoffed the Imp. 'It won't bite you.'

'We knew another stream, once,' said Jill softly.

'Yes,' said Jack. 'But it wasn't like an ordinary stream.'

'Why . . . what did it do?'

'It stood still.'* And he trembled slightly as he spoke the words.

'Well, *this* isn't an ordinary stream either,' boasted the Imp. 'It's a magic stream.'

'Oh Jill!' cried Jack. 'D'you think it's the same stream as ours?'

'It won't stand still, if that's what you mean. At least, I *hope* it won't. It would be dreadfully awkward if it did; I just can't think what the Mountain would do without it.'

'Why? What use is it to the Mountain?'

'That's just what I'm going to show you. Now stay very still and watch everything that I do.'

*

Swiftly the Imp peeled off his green gloves and stuffed them in his pocket. Then he opened the flap of his haversack and drew out something wrapped in tissue paper. Very gently he folded back the tissue paper, and as he did so, the whole cave glowed in a most beautiful silver light.

* See *The Stream that Stood Still*, by Beverley Nichols.

For a moment Jill was so dazzled by the light that she did not realize where it came from. Then she saw that it flowed from yet another pair of gloves, sparkling on the paper before them.

'Oh, what *wonderful* gloves!' she exclaimed.

'It almost hurts to look at them,' said Jack, blinking his eyes. 'What are they made of?'

'Well, I don't know *everything* they're made of,' replied the Imp, 'because, of course, they're magic. But I do know that the cloth is woven by three white spiders that live on an iceberg near the North Pole. As they are the only three white spiders in the whole world, and as they're all getting rather old, and as they only weave their webs at night, when the moon is very bright, naturally the cloth is very difficult to come by.'

He began to draw the gloves on.

'I'd *love* to wear them, just for once,' sighed Jill.

'I'm afraid you mustn't do that because they'd freeze your hands. Just feel!'

Gently she touched one of the gloves, and drew back her finger with a scream.

'It's like ice.'

The Imp nodded. 'I told you so. In fact these diamond buttons *are* carved out of ice, and the embroidery on the back is real frost. Only it's so much colder than ordinary frost that it wouldn't melt even if you put it in the fire.'

He gave a last pat to the gloves. Then he re-opened his haversack, and drew out another little bundle of tissue paper. And now the cave was flooded with an even more brilliant light, and the children saw that this time it came from a tiny key that lay on the paper, sparkling like a jewel.

'That key's made from ice, too,' the Imp told them . . . 'the iciest ice in the whole world. The Mountain once told me that a whole huge iceberg had been ground up to make it. That's why I have to wear these gloves when I touch it. If I didn't, I'd be turned into an icicle in no time. Now watch.'

He slid the key into a panel in the rock, and turned it

69

round. As he did so, the children heard a sudden increase in the flow of the waters above; instead of a gentle burbling there was a swift roar and rush, as though the waters had broken their bounds and were hurtling down towards them through the rocks. Closer and closer came the sound, and Jill looked around her wildly, seeking some place of escape, for she feared that in a moment the waters would burst through.

'It's all right,' cried the Imp. 'Don't be frightened. Follow me!'

He sprang down from the ledge, and grasped the children's hands. They slid down after him.

'Now you've got to run with me as quickly as you can, and I promise you'll see something!'

They scurried down a long winding corridor that made Jill think of the inside of a snake. As they twisted and turned it became hotter and hotter, and brighter and brighter, as though they were running straight towards a furnace.

Suddenly the Imp tugged sharply at their hands, and they all stopped, panting with the heat. 'It's just round the corner,' he breathed. 'And you'd better shield your eyes, because it's pretty scorching. Now!'

They crept round the edge, and as they did so the children's hearts stood still. For a few moments all they could see was a great whirling mist of fiery red, that seemed to go on for ever. Then, as their eyes became accustomed to the glare, they realized that they were staring down into a vast, boiling crater. It is difficult to describe exactly what they saw, because no human eyes have ever looked on such a scene before, but perhaps you may get a faint idea of it if you try to imagine that you were a tiny fly perched on the edge of a huge saucepan, and that you were looking down into the boiling, bubbling water from which clouds of steam were rising. But in this case, instead of the steam being white, it was coloured a fierce pink by the flames that lit up the bottom of the crater, and instead of the smooth sides of the saucepan, there were wild, jagged cliffs, red and angry, that seemed

They were staring down into a vast boiling crater

to stretch into the farthest distances. It was a sight that might well have filled the heart of any grown-up with awe, and the two children crouched there, speechless.

'It's all right . . . don't worry . . . it's really all right!' The Imp had to shout to make himself heard above the hiss of the steam and the growling of the scalding rocks. 'Just wait a minute!'

Even as he spoke, from close beside him, came the loudest hiss of all, and as the children sharply turned their heads, they saw, pouring from a hole in the rock by their sides, a silver jet of ice-cold water. It shot out into space, like an arrow, and then it fell, down . . . down . . . till it was lost to sight. But as it fell, the clouds of steam around it slowly began to turn from an angry pink to a clear cool white. And every moment that the dancing water descended, the air became cooler, the cliffs lost their angry flush, and the clouds of steam drifted away, leaving – instead of a boiling crater – a vast, dark quarry, lit only by an occasional flicker of flame from the far depths, where the water had not yet reached.

The Imp looked at them with a grin. 'Quick work, eh? And now we must go back, and turn the key again, and stop the water.' He rose to his feet to go.

But the children were still staring with wide eyes into the great, dark space before them.

'It's wonderful,' whispered Jill. 'But I still don't understand. Where are we? What is it?'

'Yes,' asked Jack, pointing out ahead of him. 'What *is* it?'

'What *is* it?' echoed the Imp. 'Do you mean to say you haven't guessed? Why . . . it's the Mountain's stomach!'

With which, he turned, and led the bewildered children back the same way that they had come.

Half an hour later, when they had climbed back to the fresh air and the sunlight, and locked the Mountain door behind them, the two children sat down on the grass, and listened to the Imp telling them one of the strangest stories they had ever heard.

'Yes,' he began, 'what you have just seen is the Mountain's stomach, and I shouldn't think that any Humans had ever seen it before.'

'But is the Mountain a . . . a person?' asked Jill.

Even as she spoke, there was a faint, dull growl, far below. The children started in alarm, but the Imp shook his head, smiling. '*That* didn't mean anything. He was just chuckling to himself.'

'Then is the Mountain a *man*?' demanded Jack. 'I mean, is there a great big giant somewhere down inside?'

The Imp shook his head. 'No. It isn't like that at all. The Mountain isn't exactly a man. And there certainly isn't anybody down inside. Nobody could live there for long. I suppose you'd say the Mountain was a sort of spirit.'

'But He gets angry like a man,' suggested Jill.

'And He gets hurt, too,' added Jack. 'When I drove the tent-pole into the earth . . .'

'For heaven's sake don't remind Him of that,' warned the Imp, 'or He *will* get angry. Anyway, who wouldn't get angry, having tent poles dug into them? However, I'm glad you mentioned that, because it brings me to what I wanted to tell you about Him. Now please listen very carefully.

'You asked me if the Mountain was a man. Well, the answer is "no", if by a "man" you mean anything like an ordinary Human, even the most enormous giant. But in a sort of way He *is* a Person. At any rate, there are quite a lot of things about Him which are almost human. And one of them is . . . indigestion!'

Jill was so astonished by this unexpected piece of news that she could only stare. But Jack suddenly giggled, and cried: 'Why, that's what Grannie gets!'

'Perhaps it is,' observed the Imp, in severe tones. 'But don't you laugh at it, because it's most unpleasant and one day you may get it yourself.'

'I'm sorry,' said Jack. 'Please go on.'

'Well,' he continued, 'now and then something happens which makes the Mountain angry. For instance, He may think that the animals aren't treating him with proper respect. I remember that once there was quite a hullabaloo when hundreds of rabbits suddenly decided to change their burrows, and started digging away like mad in the soft earth on the South side. You might almost have thought the Mountain was ticklish by the fuss He made. And then, He gets upset by the Clerk of the Weather. The clerk's growing very old now, and he's always making mistakes. He once ordered so much snow that the Mountain was almost suffocated, and quite often he forgets to send any rain, and the Mountain gets thirsty. All sorts of things may happen to annoy the Mountain, and when they do – well, He gets indigestion. All hot and bubbly inside, as though He wanted to burst.'

'Like . . . like a volcano?' suggested Jill.

'I don't know what a volcano is, but I do know that there's only one cure for it. And that's the stream. Whenever the Mountain feels so uncomfortable inside that He can't bear it any longer, He sends me a message . . .'

'How does He send it?'

'Ah – that's my secret! Anyway, I get the message, and whatever I'm doing I have to leave it, and hurry along, just as we've been doing now, and climb down through the caves, and put on my magic gloves, and turn the ice-key in the lock. And as soon as I do that, the stream up above changes its course, and plunges down through a secret passage which leads to the Mountain's stomach. When it gets there . . . well, you saw what happened. It's like a sort of soothing medicine, which takes away the fever and makes the Mountain feel comfortable again, so that He can go to sleep. So now you know everything!'

There was a moment's silence while the children pondered on all that the Imp had told them.

'I think it's the most wonderful story I ever heard,' said Jack, at length.

'So do I,' said Jill. 'Much the most wonderful.' She sighed and shook her head.

'How quiet it is, all of a sudden,' said Jack. 'Do you think the Mountain is asleep now?'

For answer the Imp bent down and put his ear to the earth. He stayed there for a few seconds; then he looked up and nodded.

'Yes,' he said. 'He's fast asleep. If you put your ear close

74

to the ground you'll hear Him snoring.'

The children bent down, but though they listened very carefully they could hear nothing.

'That comes of being Human, I expect,' chuckled the Imp.

'Never mind,' said Jill. 'All that matters is that He *is* asleep. And I do hope that He doesn't wake up again, not for a long time.'

To which Jack added a fervent 'So do I!'

10. Plot and Counterplot

The Imp was sad and worried.

As the days went by, and as the news of the Treasure Trove spread all over the Mountain, he felt more and more shut out of things. Nobody could talk of anything but the Treasure Trove, and since he had not had anything to do with it, and could not imagine where it could be, and since, indeed, he hated the whole idea, because he felt that it was coming between him and the children, he was left alone to sulk in his little cave, and it was seldom that anybody came near him.

Sometimes he felt so depressed that he wanted to sit down and cry. He could, of course, have made a pilgrimage to the summit of the Mountain, and have asked Him for His help, but that was something which he did not feel at all inclined to do. Whenever he wanted to speak directly to the Mountain, he had to go without food for several days beforehand, and then he had to go into a magic trance, and it was all very tiring and difficult. Besides, this was the time of the year when the Mountain was beginning

His long winter sleep; and He would have been moved to an awful anger if He were disturbed for anything less than a crisis. And the Imp did not think that this business of the Treasure Trove could possibly be described as a crisis, however much he himself might hate it.

Had he known what the witch was doing, at that very moment, he might have been of a very different opinion.

*

Miss Smith was standing on the edge of the cliff, in front of the children's tent, looking out over the valley. She had decided that it was time to tell the children about the glider. If they responded as she hoped – if they were really excited about the idea – she would send Sam down into the valley to start building it that very night.

So she turned to the children and said: 'What a beautiful view this is. It is so beautiful that it makes me wish I could fly!'

'Me too!' echoed Jill.

'And me . . . and me!' cried Jack, clapping his hands.

'Just think of it,' continued the witch. 'How wonderful it would be, just to be able to spread out your arms, and lean forward, and take a deep breath, and then give a little jump, and float, float out into the air.'

'Like a seagull!' cried Jack, spreading out his arms and tiptoeing nearer the edge.

'Careful!' Jill caught him by the hand. 'Not too near!'

Miss Smith stood behind them, grinding her sharp nails into the palms of her hands; it was only with the greatest difficulty that she could resist the temptation to give them both a push which would send them hurtling into space. But she controlled herself.

'Yes,' she said, 'one could sway about in the wind, as if one were a bird, and hover in the air, and swoop down, and up again, just as one felt inclined . . .'

Jack jumped up and down. 'Oh, how lovely it sounds!'

'And farther down the cliff,' she added, 'where no little boy could ever climb, there are all sorts of beautiful fruits that you could pick when you were flying. Apricots and peaches and melons, all ripe and waiting to be eaten!'

'Oh, please don't go on like that . . . I can hardly bear it!' shouted Jack. 'It makes me want to jump over right away.'

Miss Smith clenched her teeth together, so strongly did she wish that he *would* jump over. But she must not be too hasty.

'No, my dear,' she said. 'Not right away. But later on, perhaps.'

'Oh, but *never*!' Jill shook her head violently. 'He must *never* think of such a thing.'

'You little darling,' crooned Miss Smith. 'Of course he mustn't. Nor must you.' And she chucked her under the chin with a finger which seemed to Jill strangely cold. 'But one day, perhaps . . .'

'One day what?' demanded Jack.

'One day we might all fly together.'

'In an aeroplane?'

'Not exactly in an aeroplane.'

'Then how?'

'In a glider.'

'A glider! But wherever should we get one?'

'Ah! That's a secret!'

'Please . . . please tell us,' entreated Jack.

'I really shouldn't. But if you promise not to tell anyone else . . .'

'We promise . . . we promise!'

'Very well. It's like this. My husband, Mr Smith, has been working day and night trying to find this Treasure Trove. I just can't *tell* you how he works; no wizard ever worked so hard before, mixing things up and boiling them in that old cauldron.

'Well,' she went on, 'last night he got much nearer than he ever got before. He doesn't know *exactly* where it is, but he *does* know that it's in a very lonely valley that nobody ever visits because the rocks are so huge and the cliffs are so steep. It would take ages and ages to reach it in the ordinary way, so what does he do? He decides to build a glider, and he's going to start this very night! What do you think of that?'

There was no need to ask the children what they thought of it; they were breathless with excitement.

'May we fly in it too?' pleaded Jack.

'Of course you may, my dears,' replied the witch, 'as soon as we know it is quite, quite safe.'

'Will it be a magic glider?' asked Jill.

'Everything my husband makes is magic,' returned the witch, 'but it will be made of the very best materials. And now you really must not ask me any more questions, for it is growing dark, and it is high time that I went home.'

The children bade Miss Smith a reluctant good night, and then, hand in hand, they ran off, still chatting eagerly of the great adventure that lay before them.

Had they turned to wave at her, at that moment, they might have had a shock. For they would have seen her standing there, a thin, black figure with the dying sunlight behind her, and they would have realized to their horror that she was no longer standing on the *edge* of the cliff, but that she had stepped *over* it, and was floating in mid-air, like a big black bird, looking back at them with an expression of indescribable hatred on her face.

*

When the witch returned to the cave she joined Sam by the fireside.

'Well,' she said, 'I've done the most I can for the moment. I've made them all crazy about the idea of the glider. The next step's to build it, and that's up to you. I think you ought to start off early tomorrow morning.'

'That's OK by me,' growled Sam, who, to tell the truth, was glad of any excuse to escape from her company.

'There's only one thing that bothers me,' said the witch, 'and that's the Imp.'

'What about him?'

'He's our enemy.'

'Pooh! A kid like that? Why, I could squash him in a couple of seconds; I could squeeze the life out of him with one hand.'

'Maybe you could, and maybe you couldn't. But there's more in that brat than meets the eye. He's got something they call the Key of the Mountain. Don't ask me what it is, but I've a feeling it's important. There's Something *inside* this old Mountain . . . Something or Somebody . . . and the Imp's the only person who knows what it is.'

'Something or Somebody!' scoffed Sam. 'Cut it out! You're seeing things!'

'It's the things I *don't* see that worry me,' returned the witch, 'and there are plenty of them in this part of the world. Sometimes, when I've been out walking, just before it's growing dark, I've *heard* things coming from down below.'

Sam gave a contemptuous laugh. 'You've heard your own shoes squeaking, that's what it is.'

She shrugged her shoulders. 'Have it your own way. All I'm telling you is that the Imp's our enemy, and it'll pay us to keep on the right side of him. If he were to guess what we were up to . . .'

She had not time to finish the sentence. For at that moment the jackdaw swept through the entrance to the cave in a state of great agitation.

'What is it?' cried the witch. 'What's the matter?'

'It's the Imp!' he panted. 'He's coming down to call on you.'

'What . . . tonight?'

'He'll be here in five minutes. And I don't like the look in his eye!'

*

It was quite true that the Imp had a very strange look in his eye as he hurried down the Mountain path, but it was not a look of anger so much as of fear. Yes, for the first time in his life he was frightened, and the worst of it was that he did not really know what he was frightened about.

When he had called on the children, an hour before, and had heard the story of the glider, his first impulse had been to share their excitement, and to ask if he might join them on their first trip. And then, little by little, as they told him more about it, he began to be worried.

All sorts of disturbing questions cropped up in his mind. Was it safe? Who would be responsible if anything went wrong? Above all, *why* should Mr and Mrs Smith have told the children anything whatever about it? That was what he could not understand. After all, it was their Treasure Trove; they were the people who were doing all the work and taking all the trouble; and from what he had seen of Sam and the witch, they did not strike him as the sort of people who would put themselves out merely to benefit somebody else.

And always, at the back of his mind, was another question, which he hardly dared to put into words, for it was prompted by pure jealousy. When the Smiths had found the Treasure Trove, was it not almost certain that they would leave the Mountain, and take the children with them? The children had hinted as much when he was talking to them. Jill had said how wonderful it would be to give a whole sack of rubies to her mother, and Jack had said that when he had his pockets full of gold he would go to a big city and buy a glider of his very own.

That was the real cause of the Imp's mistrust of Sam and the witch; they might take his new friends away from him. Already, with all this talk of the Treasure Trove, the children had forgotten the marvels he had shown them on that great day when they had visited the Mountain's heart. And when the treasure was found, they would all depart, and leave him once more on the Mountain, solitary and sad, with only the animals to talk to.

At all costs, he felt, that must be prevented. How, he did not know. But he was a brave little boy, and that was the reason why he was now on his way to the witch's cave, to spy out the land.

*

Inside the cave all was confusion. Sam and the witch and the jackdaw were rushing round in circles, trying to make everything look neat and homely before the Imp arrived, tidying things up and putting things away. Soon the last traces of witchery had disappeared. Miss Smith flopped into a chair with a sigh of relief.

'That's that,' she said. 'Everything looks fine. But you'd better put on your wizard's cap.'

Sam reached for it, and stuck it on his head. It made him feel a fool, but since he was supposed to be a wizard he might as well play the part.

'There's still a minute or so before he comes,' said the witch. 'I think I'll put Mr Jackdaw through his paces. It's very important for him to make a good impression. Mr Jackdaw, come here!'

Mr Jackdaw hopped obediently over.

'Now listen, my dear,' she warned him, waving a skinny finger in front of his eyes. 'When this nasty little boy comes in, you must remember that you're supposed to have reformed.'

'Reformed,' squawked the wicked bird.

'And that you wouldn't steal a cent.'

'Not a cent,' echoed the lying creature.

'So tell me what you'd say if he accused you of being a thief. What would you say? Show me!'

The jackdaw cleared his throat, took a step backwards, and closed his eyes for a moment, to remember the lesson she had taught him. Then he began, in a pleading, whining tone . . .

'Oh, Your Royal Highness, how can you *say* such things? And me trying to go straight at last, after all these years! I wouldn't pinch a penny, no I wouldn't, Your Royal Highness; it would be wicked, that's what Mrs Smith told me, it would be downright wicked, and I want to be good . . . I want to be good . . . I want to be go . . . o . . . o . . . d!'

The witch clapped her hands in delight.

'Splendid!' she cried. 'You did it so beautifully that you almost make me believe you mean it.' A sudden dreadful thought crossed her mind. 'You *don't* mean it, do you?'

'Of course I don't,' he protested indignantly.

'You'd steal the ring off a dead man's finger, wouldn't you?'

'I would! I would!' squawked the deplorable bird.

'You'd steal the pennies out of a blind man's bowl, wouldn't you?'

'I would! I would! And when I'd stolen them I'd come back and give him an extra tweak on the nose!'

The witch was enchanted by this little refinement. 'That's a good bird. Just you keep that spirit and you'll never go wrong.'

Even as she spoke, the shadow of the Imp fell across the threshold.

For a moment Miss Smith pretended not to have noticed him.

'Keep that spirit and you'll never go wrong,' she repeated. Then she gave a start, and turned. 'Why, if it isn't Master Imp! You've caught me just when I was giving Mr Jackdaw his lessons.'

She rose to her feet and welcomed him.

'I was just passing, so I thought I'd look in.'

'Well, I *do* think that's nice,' crooned the witch. 'Isn't it, Sam?'

'Eh – what's that?' said Sam, who was sitting over the fire, balancing his wizard's cap over one eye.

'You mustn't mind him,' whispered the witch, with a little giggle. 'Whenever he put on his wizard's cap, he gets very absent-minded, and just sits there, weaving spells and dreaming dreams.'

'What does he dream about?' asked the Imp.

'Oh, the most beautiful things. Usually it's sweet-smelling flowers and tiny little babies. You've no idea the lovely things he dreams about. I quite envy him sometimes.' Which was, of course, a howling lie, for if ever there was one thing which Miss Smith hated more than a sweet-smelling flower, it was a tiny little baby; the very sight of one made her feel quite sick.

'Do sit down,' she entreated. 'I expect you've come to talk about the Treasure Trove.'

'Well, in a way, I had. You see . . . in my position . . .'

'Of course,' she interrupted. 'Very important. Must know what's going on. I quite agree.'

The Imp was surprised to find her so co-operative.

'There's only one thing that worries me about the Treasure Trove,' she went on. And here she fixed him with a look so cunning that Sam and the jackdaw both cocked their ears in her direction, for they guessed that she was going to say something very important.

'What's that?' asked the Imp.

'The *time* it will take. It's so huge that we may need years even to sort it out. Mayn't we, Sam?'

'Years and years and years,' he agreed, guessing that this was what she wanted him to say.

'But why should that worry you?' demanded the Imp.

'Oh, I'm not thinking of *myself*,' declared Miss Smith. 'I never think of myself, do I, Mr Jackdaw?'

'No,' squawked that black-hearted creature. 'She never thinks of herself.'

'No. It's those sweet children I'm thinking of. You see, I'm afraid that once we've found the Trove, they'll never want to go home again.'

She paused to let the full effect of her words sink in. And that they *had* sunk in was clear from the flush that came to the Imp's cheeks and the eager light that shone in his eyes.

'Why do you think that?' he asked, trying to keep his voice from trembling.

'Well, it's obvious, isn't it? They're both terribly keen and excited about the whole thing. And if we make them partners, as we certainly shall, nothing will persuade them to leave the Mountain till it's all settled.'

She paused again, watching the Imp. Yes, she had certainly struck the right note. For he was saying to himself that at all costs, now, he must help forward the scheme of the Treasure Trove. If it really meant that Jack and Jill – and especially Jill – would stay on the Mountain for years, maybe for ever, it would be the most wonderful stroke of luck that had ever happened.

'I'd like to help you,' he stammered, at length.

'Do you think you should?' taunted the witch. 'After all, they *ought* to be going home again quite soon; their mother will be expecting them, and I'm afraid she may scold me terribly for keeping them.'

'Perhaps it won't take as long as you think,' returned the Imp, sincerely hoping that it would take even longer. 'Anyway, we must certainly go ahead.'

'Well, if you insist . . .' sighed the witch, pretending that he was persuading her. Then she gave a gay little laugh. 'And now that that's settled, may I offer you some refreshment?'

'I really ought to be going,' said the Imp, reaching for his green hat.

'It's been a lovely visit,' she crooned. 'And I'm so glad you made it because sometimes I wondered if we really were friends.'

The Imp gulped; he still felt uneasy at the idea of being friends with this strange person. However, fate seemed to have decided that this was how it was to be, so he must make the best of it. He held out his hand.

'We are friends,' he echoed.

But as he shook her hand he wondered. Although it was so prettily manicured and powdered, with gleaming nails and a fragrant scent, it felt like the hand of a toad . . . it felt like dead, wet nettles in the rain. He suppressed a shudder and forced a smile. A moment later he was gone.

The witch sat down heavily upon the bed. 'If I have much more of this I shall scream,' she snapped.

'Much more of what?' demanded Sam.

'Being nice. I don't want to be nice. I want to be nasty, I want to be very nasty indeed.'

'So do I,' he growled. 'That's why I'll be glad to get down to work.'

'And about time too.'

11. Peril in the Sky

It was barely dawn when Sam set out for the valley, on his way to the wreck of the aeroplane from which he planned to build a glider. The moon was still riding in a cloudless sky, and it shone through the entrance of the cave, lighting up the thin features of Miss Smith, who was still sleeping, and outlining the figure of the skeleton with a ghastly glow, so that it seemed as though the great empty eye sockets were staring at him, watching his every movement.

Sam had been prepared to travel well into the following night, but when he was half way down the Mountain, he had a piece of luck. He came upon a stray Shetland pony that was grazing by the side of the path, and with a single leap he landed on its back, and dug his sharp heels into its flanks. Poor little pony!

When Sam at last reached the wreckage, he dismounted, and hobbled one of the pony's legs to a rock, giving him a sharp kick as he did so, just to show him who was master. Then he turned and looked about him. And as he did so, his face grew grim, for the aeroplane was far more badly damaged than he had expected. Rusty pieces of the engine were strewn far and wide, most of the metal-work was warped and twisted, and the fabric was in such a state of decay that long strips of it hung loose, and fluttered mournfully in the breeze.

To add to the desolation of the scene, some giant vultures had made their nest in the cockpit. As soon as they saw him approaching, they flew out with angry cries, and crouched on the broken wings, where they stayed watching him, black and hunchbacked, with their cruel beaks clattering as though they would like to tear him asunder.

'Soon put a stop to that,' muttered Sam, drawing his pistol from his belt. He took aim and fired; the largest of the vultures flopped dead in the sand, and the others, screaming hoarsely, rose into the air with a flurry of black wings. Higher and higher they flew, till they were like tiny black spots in the heavens. But from time to time the black spots would grow bigger again, and Sam knew that they were still watching him, and would continue to do so till he had gone. So his hand never strayed very far from his pistol.

After a brief examination of the plane, his spirits began to rise, for he found that in spite of the damage, there would still be enough material from which he could build a new machine. So he got to work with a will, intent on seeing how much of the plane he would be able to strip, and load on to the pony's back before the sun went down.

And there we will leave him, in the fading light, clambering in and out of the giant skeleton of the plane, with the vultures hovering overhead.

It would be nice to be able to tell you that he failed in his purpose, that the vultures got him, or that he fell over a cliff on the way back. However, this is a true story, and we have to tell you that nothing of that sort happened. Everything went well with him, all too well; and a few days later, after three more journeys up and down the Mountain – journeys in which he nearly broke the poor little pony's back with the mass of material which he piled upon it – the first part of his task was completed, and he and the witch were able to sit down, and begin to hammer their evil machine into shape.

*

At last the glider was finished, and one sunny morning Sam and the witch towed it up to an ideal place for testing it – a gentle sandy slope half way between their cave and the children's tent. It needed only a few trials to prove that Sam had done a first-rate job; it dipped and soared with absolute precision, and it answered to the lightest touch of the controls. So perfect was it that the witch was quite worried.

'I suppose you *will* be able to make it go wrong, when the time comes?' she demanded.

'No fear of that,' rejoined Sam. 'Just a question of loosening one or two of the screws.'

'Well, I only hope you're right. A nice pair of fools we should look, if we found that we'd gone to all this trouble just to give them a joy-ride.'

They decided that they would start the children off gradually, to get them used to it. 'Just a few yards the first time,' said the witch, 'then a bit more, and then for quite long flights, before we send them off on the last flight – THE flight.'

When, on that first afternoon, Jill stood at the top of the slope and watched Jack clamber into the seat, pull the lever, and sail gently into the air, coming to rest a minute later in the soft sand below, all her misgivings left her.

'Was it fun?' she asked eagerly, as Jack climbed back up the slope.

'Oh, Jill, it was glorious! Just like flying. You *must* try it.'

Jill could not resist any longer. 'All right, I will! But it must be a very little one.'

Sam came up to them, pulling the glider after him. 'Changed your mind?' he asked, when he saw Jill step forward. 'Good! Jump in!'

Jill climbed into the seat.

'Sure you know what to do? Then off we go!'

She pulled the handle, and the machine darted forward like a bird. Oh, but this was the loveliest feeling she had ever known, drifting swiftly and silently through the air, with the breeze on her face, and the green branches dancing by below! She gave a turn to the handle, and the glider immediately obeyed her, catching the wind, and mounting ever so slightly. She longed to see how far she could go, to try all sorts of twists and turns, but she must not be too rash at first. So she pushed the lever gently downwards, and the machine slowly sank, hovered for a moment, and then came to rest in the sand, with hardly any bump at all.

Jill stepped out and saw Jack scrambling down the sand-bank and running towards her.

'Wasn't it grand?' he shouted. 'Didn't you love it?'

'Oh Jack! It was much the nicest thing I've ever done.'

'And you didn't have such a little one after all – you had a much bigger one than I did. Now I'm going to try again!'

Jill was too excited to try to stop him; besides, she was longing to have another flight herself. So the two children seized the rope, and tugged the glider up the slope. They had forgotten all about Sam and the witch, who were standing in the shadow of an old yew tree watching them, grinning wickedly when they saw how well their plans were working.

'We'll leave 'em to themselves for a few days,' said Sam, 'till they get so crazy about it that they'll want to fly to the moon.'

'That's the idea,' agreed the witch. 'But instead of flying to the moon, they'll fly in a very different direction. He! he! he! Ho! ho! ho!'

*

And now came the great day when the final flight was to be be made.

If the children had only paused to think a little more clearly and to ask themselves what they were really doing, they might well have been inclined to hesitate before taking this great risk. What did they really *know* of Sam and the witch? Who *were* they? Where did they come from? What would their parents have thought of them? And again, what did the children know of the Treasure Trove? What proof had they even of its very existence? True, Sam had drawn a little map, and explained to Jack how to guide the glider – so he said – to the very entrance of the cave where it was hidden. But how could they be sure that the wizard – for that was how they regarded him – was speaking the truth? Above all, if the treasure was so valuable, why did not Sam fly down to it himself? Why did he leave it all to a couple of children?

True, from time to time Jill had her doubts, and on several occasions she had taken out the magic compass and pointed it first at the glider and then at the witch. But as it always pointed either to Peace or to Happiness, she felt that her fears were groundless, and so she put it away again. Even if it had pointed to Danger it is more than possible that she would have ignored the warning, for to tell the truth, both the children were so excited by the adventure that they could not have borne to have it interrupted.

Well, those plots had now reached their climax. All night long Sam had been working on the glider, pretending to tighten certain vital screws when, in fact, he was loosening them, assuring himself – so he said – that the controls were properly adjusted, when he was actually wrecking them. When he finally towed it to the edge of the cliff in the morning he turned to the witch and whispered:

'It's a death-trap.'

'Ho! Ho! He! He!' she cackled. 'That's what we want. A death-trap.'

And the jackdaw joined in her laughter, and flapped up and down, squawking with glee, and casting his evil eyes down to the sharp rocks so far below, where the children would soon be hurtling to their destruction.

'Ssh! They're coming!' hissed the witch.

Sure enough, the children were coming from their tent.

*

'Ready?'

The children nodded.

'Steady!'

Jack took a tighter grip of the controls.

And then, just as Sam was about to shout 'Go!' there was a hoarse cry behind them, followed by a scream from the witch, and before they knew what was happening a heavy black shape hurtled through the air, landing on their backs with such force that they were both knocked almost senseless.

For the next few seconds they hardly knew what was happening. Poor Jill lay on the ground, half-stunned, blinking up to the sky, which seemed to be full of whirling stars. Jack was knocked from his seat and rolled over and over, feeling something warm and hairy against his face, and sharp claws scratching his back; and all the time he was half deafened by screams and curses, for in the general confusion the witch had also been knocked down, and Sam had tripped up over her, and she was so furious that she had bitten him in the ankle, and they were tearing at each other like a couple of wild cats.

Suddenly the thing with which Jack had been struggling gave him a final push into the heather and leapt away.

He jumped to his feet. And as he did so, his heart filled with dismay. For he saw that the black shape which had attacked him was none other than Nero, the monkey, who at this very moment was jumping into the seat of the glider, and fumbling for the handle which would send it off into space.

'No! No!' he cried, running forward. 'That's mine! Stop thief! Stop thief!' But it was too late. The monkey turned round with a savage grin, waved goodbye, and pulled the lever. For a moment nothing happened, and then, just as Jack was upon him, the machine darted forward, and soared proudly into the air.

Jack stayed by the edge, clenching his fists, his eyes

filled with angry tears.

'It's going so beautifully,' cried Jack, with a sob in his throat. 'And I'm sure that we shall *never* see it again.'

'That's true enough,' growled Sam to the witch. 'It'll break in two at any minute now.'

'Ssh!' she whispered. 'You're a fool to say such things.' Aloud she said to the children: 'Well, darlings, it's all very sad, but at least it does go to prove what a wonderful machine Mr Smith built for you . . . so safe and sure.'

Even as she spoke, Jill gave a shrill scream. For the glider, which had been slowly drifting down in long graceful circles, suddenly seemed to pause and tremble, and then, without any more warning, it split in two. One wing shot down like a stone into the valley, the other, with the black shape of Nero clinging to the tip, fluttered madly around for a few seconds and then it too dived earthwards, and a moment later was lost to sight.

Jill covered her face with her hands. There was silence.

'Serves him right!' snarled Sam, at length, from behind them.

The witch shook her head sharply, and pointed to the children. 'We must pretend to be *sorry*,' she hissed. And aloud she said:

'Oh dear, oh dear, the *poor* little monkey! It's too terrible.' She fumbled for her handkerchief, and dabbed it on her eyes. 'Whatever made him do it?'

'He was jealous,' explained Jack, in a hushed voice. 'He always hated us, didn't he, Jill?'

For a moment Jill did not speak. She was still feeling shattered by what had happened. Then she pulled herself together.

'He certainly didn't like us very much,' she replied. 'And whenever he heard anybody mention the glider he got in a terrible rage. I suppose he wanted to fly in it himself.'

'Poor, silly, naughty little thing,' sobbed the witch, pretending to be quite overcome. 'Of course, it was very wicked of him to steal the glider like that, but . . . oh dear! oh dear! . . . what a terrible punishment!' She turned to

Sam and winked at him behind her hand. 'Whatever do you think he *did* to the glider, my dear?'

'Yes, what could he have done?' echoed Jack, turning round.

'Must have undone the centre screw,' said Sam gruffly. 'No other explanation.'

'Why, of course, that was it,' agreed the witch. 'He never could see a screw without trying to undo it.' She gave Sam another wink. 'Don't you remember, my dear, how he came round one day when we were working, and how he undid all the screws the moment our backs were turned?'

'Why, so I do!' lied Sam. 'Yes, that was what happened, beyond a doubt.'

Jill shook her head sadly. It was all very strange and very terrible. And though she supposed that 'Mr and Mrs Smith' must be right, she could not understand how an intelligent animal like Nero could possibly have been so crazy as to split the machine in half with his own hands.

'Anyway,' said Sam, turning to go home, 'we've seen the last of *him*. Come on. I'm ready for my tea.'

The witch gave a final dab to her eyes, blew the children a kiss, and then, with every appearance of grief and exhaustion, slowly followed him down the hill.

12. Tales of Treasure

If Miss Smith had not been a person of remarkable character, she might well have been acutely depressed by the failure of her glider plot. But Miss Smith was at her best when things were going against her.

And so, as she walked home with Sam to the cave, after Nero had wrecked her wicked schemes, she still held her head high, and apart from an occasional puff of green smoke which escaped from her left nostril, you would not have guessed that anything was worrying her at all.

Sam, on the other hand, was in the depths of gloom.

'Well, that's that!' he growled, throwing his wizard's cap into the corner. 'We might as well pack up and go home.'

'Go home!' echoed the jackdaw, who was looking equally dejected.

Miss Smith folded her arms, and snorted contemptuously. 'When I look at the pair of you, I feel ashamed to stay in the same cave. Where's your spirit?'

'Where's the glider?' retorted Sam.

'Who cares where the glider is? If you ask me, we're well rid of it. In fact, the whole thing's a blessing in disguise.'

Sam gaped at her open-mouthed.

'Yes,' she repeated, 'a blessing in disguise. For what would have happened if those two kids *had* crashed? It wouldn't just have ended there. Oh no! They'd have sent up a whole crowd of people from down below, nosing about and asking questions. They'd have sent lots of policemen, for instance, and if there's one thing that gives me the creeps, it's a policeman. They might even have sent the army. And they'd certainly have sent that old woman – what's her name? – the kids' grandmother. *She* knows a thing or two, I can tell you. It isn't everybody who could have made that magic compass, even though I *did* manage to fix it.'

'We could have made a get-away,' muttered Sam.

'Maybe we could and maybe we couldn't. It isn't so easy to make a get-away after you've murdered the heir to a throne. Besides, there'd have been witnesses.'

Sam made a rude face. 'Witnesses! A lot of silly animals.'

'Not so silly that they can't talk.'

'Well, whatever we do, we'll always have *them* to reckon with.'

'Shall we?'

'Of course we shall. There's no way to get rid of 'em, short of blowing up the whole Mountain.'

'Quite,' returned the witch, in a strange voice.

'What's the use of saying "quite" like that? It's true, isn't it?'

The witch nodded. 'Of course it's true. I was only trying to show that I agreed with you. There's no way of getting rid of the animals – and the kids with them – *short of blowing up the Mountain.*'

As she spoke she fixed him with a glittering eye. At last he understood.

'You don't mean . . . you don't mean you *could?*' he gasped.

95

'Why not? Not *all* of it maybe. That wouldn't be necessary. But enough of it to bury them – the whole lot of them – so deep that they wouldn't be dug up again for a hundred years.'

She stalked over to the corner, where she kept her big travelling trunk. Bending down she threw back the lid, and drew out a narrow black box, which she set on the table.

'Open it!' she said, 'and look what's inside.'

Sam opened it, and even as he did so, he staggered back in alarm.

'Dynamite!' he yelled.

'All right – it won't bite you!' scoffed the witch.

'Why didn't you tell me you carried that stuff about with you? You might have blown us all sky-high.'

'Don't be daft! It doesn't go off just by dropping it. It's got to be properly set and the fuses properly lit. However, if you're so scared, we'll put it away again.'

She took the box and put it back in the trunk. It was not till she had closed the lid that Sam and the jackdaw breathed more easily.

'Well,' she said, coming back to the fire, 'what d'you think of the plan?'

'I can't say till you've told me what the plan *is*. Blowing people up isn't a plan – it's just a pleasant dream.'

'Very well. This is how we make the dream come true. The first thing we've got to do is to find a huge cave, so huge that it'll hold the entire population of the Mountain. Got that?'

Sam nodded.

'This cave wants to have a secret exit so that we can get away in a hurry. Got that?'

'So far, so good.'

'But the *main* entrance will have to be dug by the animals.'

'Why?'

'Because we want the whole lot of 'em in there, without a single witness left outside. And because the only way we can be sure of that is to work them up to a great pitch of excitement, so that they'll all be crazy to dig their way through.'

Sam still looked puzzled.

'Use your brains,' demanded the witch impatiently. 'Supposing you were one of those wretched creatures, and you were told that by digging through part of the hillside you could find a treasure, wouldn't you dig like mad?'

'Yes. But if there's another entrance all the time . . .'

'It'll be a *secret* entrance, you silly. They won't know about it. It's only *we* who'll know about it. When they're all inside, we can block up the tunnel the animals have dug, set the fuses for the dynamite, creep out through our own private way, and then . . . stand back and watch the fun!'

She rubbed her hands with glee; a wicked grin spread slowly over Sam's face; and the jackdaw hopped up and down on his perch, squawking with excitement.

And then the witch put up a warning finger. 'But don't let's count our chickens before they're hatched,' she said.

'We've still got a long way to go. We've got to find the right place, and that may take some doing. In the meantime, we've got to make sure the animals don't lose interest. Most important of all, we've got to avoid doing anything that might arouse the suspicions of those two brats, and their friend the Imp. Which reminds me . . .' and here she turned to the jackdaw . . . 'I want you to go up to their tent one night very soon and steal that compass again. I don't want to run any risks of them mending it.'

'Can I steal anything else?' demanded the jackdaw eagerly.

'Yes, my darling. Anything you like, provided that nobody sees you.'

By now, the general feeling in the cave was very much more cheerful, with the prospect of so many busy, happy days ahead. And without any more ado, they all three of them sat down at the table and began to work out their plans in detail.

*

The witch had been right. The animals had been deeply disturbed by the disaster of the glider. But it was in the children's tent that the matter was most earnestly discussed. For hours on end Jack and Jill sat round the fire, talking about the strange tangle of events in which they had become involved, and often at these meetings they were joined by the Imp.

'What do *you* think we should do?' demanded Jack.

The question put the Imp in a very difficult position. At his interview with Sam and the witch he had been persuaded that the only way to keep the children on the Mountain was by keeping them searching for the treasure. Yet he did not really feel happy about such a plan not only because he did not trust the Smiths, but also because he had an uneasy suspicion that perhaps there might not be any treasure at all.

So he did not know what he ought to reply to Jack's question. For a moment his better nature triumphed.

'Sometimes I wonder whether we shouldn't forget all about it,' he suggested.

Both the children looked at him in astonishment. 'But if we do forget all about it,' said Jill, 'that means that we ought to start to think of going home.'

'And the holiday's only just begun,' protested Jack.

Jill smiled. 'It may feel like that, but we've been up here quite a while. And we promised not to stay too long.'

The Imp sighed; he was afraid that the witch had been right, after all. 'Does this old treasure mean so very much to you?' he asked, with a touch of bitterness in his voice.

'Not to me; but it would mean a great deal to Mummy and Daddy.'

'I understand,' said the Imp. He did not really understand at all; but at least he saw that he must do all he could to forward the idea of the treasure hunt.

'Well, if that's the case,' he said, rising to his feet, 'supposing we go out right away, and start exploring?'

'That's a lovely idea,' cried Jack, springing up at once and leaving them to put on his climbing boots.

Soon Jill heard Jack's voice calling to her from the tent.

Sat round the fire talking

There she found Jack staring at Mr Caterpillar, who was stretched out on a big green leaf on the camp bed.

'I don't like the look of him at all,' said Jack.

'What is it, my dear?' asked Jill, bending over the caterpillar, and touching him very gently with her finger. 'Oh dear! He's so hot! And he's trembling all over!'

The caterpillar answered in a tiny squeak that seemed very faint and far away. 'I'm all right,' he gasped.

'No, you're *not* all right,' rejoined Jill. 'You've got a fever.'

'Is . . . is that all it is?'

'Of course.'

The caterpillar gave a deep sigh and his trembling became less violent.

'Thank you,' he said. 'I was afraid . . . afraid that . . .'

'Afraid that what?'

'Afraid that perhaps . . .' and here his voice sank to the faintest whisper '. . . I might be turning into a chrys . . . chrys . . .'

But he was so exhausted that he could not finish the sentence.

Jill put her finger to her lips. 'He's fallen asleep,' she whispered. 'That's much the best thing that could have happened. He'll feel much better when he wakes up.'

So they all went off down the hill together, laughing in the sunshine.

13. The Kidnapped Caterpillar

It was nearly dark when Jill returned to the tent, having left the two boys down in the valley, exploring some small caves that they had found near a bend in the river. They had promised that they would come home some time that night, but in spite of this, she felt tired and lonely, and – for some reason which she could not define – upset by all sorts of vague fears and forebodings.

She sighed, and said to herself: 'I mustn't let my imagination run away with me. Of course everything is all right. I'll get the supper ready and make a nice fire to warm them in case I'm asleep when they return.'

Soon the table was laid, and outside, in the shelter of the rock a beautiful fire of logs was blazing merrily away, sending golden shadows flickering among the dark branches of the pines.

Then Jill bethought herself of the caterpillar. 'Oh dear,' she murmured, 'how could I be so unkind as to forget about him when he is ill? Whatever will he think of me, not going in to see him?'

She hurried back to the tent, and went straight over to the camp-bed where the cabbage leaf was lying, with the poplar leaf on top of it. Very gently she lifted the top leaf, smiling as she remembered how they had all laughed at the thought of him eating his own bedclothes.

And then the smile faded. The caterpillar had gone!

Whatever had happened to him? He certainly shouldn't have got out of bed with such a heavy fever; he would only make it worse. 'Caterpillar! Caterpillar!' she called, raising her voice so that it sounded high above the crackling of the logs outside. But there was no reply.

Then suddenly she smiled to herself. How silly she was! Of course, he was fast asleep – that was what it was! He had just crawled off the leaf, and curled up somewhere in a corner, out of the way, and she hadn't noticed him because it was growing so dark. So she ran back and lit the lamp. Even as she did so, a tiny object lying on the table met her eyes. It was dark brown and shrivelled like a bean. She put out her finger to touch it and then, with a gasp of dismay, she stepped back.

Could it be what she thought it was? Was it possible? Oh, caterpillar – caterpillar – has it happened after all? Have you turned into a chrysalis?

With tears in her eyes, she bent forward once again, and peered at the tiny thing, so still, so lifeless. Yes, it was all too true. It was indeed a chrysalis. And as though to remove her last doubts, there, by the side of the lamp, lay a letter, rapidly scrawled, as if the writer had been in terrible haste to finish it. Yes, it was indeed from him, for it was written in those thick, inky words which were all he could manage, since he could only write by sitting on the edge of the inkpot and dipping his tail into it. She took it up, brushed away her tears, and read . . .

DEAR PRINCESS JILL,
    It has begun to happen. I am TURNING. I cannot stop it, however hard I try. First it was my lower legs, and

then it was my back, and now there is a hateful sort of skin creeping all over me, so that I can hardly move.

I am so frightened. If only you had been here you might have stopped it. But now it is too late. The skin is growing tighter every minute, my eyes are growing heavier, I can feel the darkness coming over me.

Please, Princess Jill, look after me when I am a chrysalis. I shall not be able to thank you because I shall be shut up tight inside this dreadful prison. But please, please, take care of me, and put me away safely in a drawer or somewhere out of the way, and please, if you ever have a moment, come and stroke me. Perhaps I may just be able to feel the touch of your finger . . .

And now I must stop. The skin is creeping over me faster and faster. Oh please, dearest Princess, remember me, and one day if I ever come out again, help me to fly back into your life as a butterfl . . .

And there the writing stopped. The last word was a long smudge which she could hardly read, like this . . .

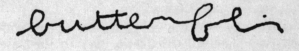

*

It was in vain that Jill tried to stop herself from weeping when she had read this letter, for it seemed to her the saddest letter that could ever have been written in the whole world. She thought of the poor frightened caterpillar, alone and trembling, with nobody to comfort him in his ordeal, feeling as though he were gradually being walled up inside a tomb, struggling to escape from the fate which was closing round him, strangling his body, sealing his eyes . . . oh, it was terrible!

Then, little by little, she realized that it was foolish to give way to such feelings. What was done was done, and there was no way to undo it. The caterpillar had turned into a chrysalis, and that was an end of it. Besides, as likely as not he was now feeling quite happy and comfortable, asleep inside his shell, and was dreaming beautiful dreams of the sunshine and the summer when he would flutter back into her life as a butterfly.

Yes, she decided, that was the way to look at it. She had lost one friend, but soon she would gain another. So she dried her eyes, stretched out her finger towards the chrysalis, and gave it a stroke. It was the very softest of strokes, for she did not want to wake him up; the more soundly he slept the sooner he would be out again.

And now . . . where to put him? It must be somewhere very special, where there could be no risk of anybody disturbing him.

Then she thought of the very place – the little gold pot-pourri case which her granny had given her before she left the Palace. It was shaped like a shell, the lid was pierced to let in the air, and it was filled with the fragrant petals of dried flowers – roses and wild thyme and lavender, with magic cloves and tiny grains of incense. Yes, that would be the softest bed that any chrysalis could ever lie on; it would be like a magic carpet which would float him away on the sweetest dreams.

She tiptoed over to the chrysalis, very gently took him between two fingers, carried him over to the case, lifted the lid, and set him to rest on the flowers.

Even as she did so, she turned round with a sudden start, for she thought that she heard a tap on the celluloid window of the tent. But there was nothing. No doubt it was the wind, which was rising fast.

She lowered the lid, stepped back and blew a kiss.

'Good night, my darling,' she whispered. 'Sleep well . . . and happy dreams!'

And now, she thought, I really feel so tired that I would like to rest a little myself. So she went out, threw a few more logs on the fire, and curled up in the shadow of the great pine tree. Then she gave a deep sigh, and a moment later she was fast asleep.

*

And now . . . where to put him?

Deeper and deeper she slept. The minutes crept on apace, the moon rose high in the heavens, sometimes shining bright, sometimes darkened by the clouds that the wind blew across it, like tattered rags. All sorts of strange shadows flickered round Jill as she slept, black and gold and green and silver.

But there was one shadow that was darker than all the rest, a shadow that did not flicker but stayed very still, as though it were watching her, a shadow with a curious shape – the shape of a bird. And it was indeed a bird. It was the wicked jackdaw. And it was his beak, tapping on the window, that Jill had heard a little while before, when she had been placing the chrysalis in its box.

Still as death the jackdaw stayed there, high up in the branches of the pine tree, his tiny green eyes fixed steadily on the figure below. He did not mind waiting – he was used to it; like all thieves a large part of his life was spent in waiting, outside windows, outside doors, waiting till honest folk had gone away and left him free to rob them.

But now he decided that he had waited long enough. Opening his wings he fluttered silently down, hovering for a moment over Jill to make sure that she was really asleep. Then, with a single swoop, he flew through the opening of the tent and perched on the table by the side of the case where the chrysalis was hidden.

So it was in there, this thing that Jill had made so much fuss about! It must obviously be very precious, for she would not put anything cheap or common in such a beautiful case. The jackdaw knew a good thing when he saw it, and this case was a good thing and no mistake. Solid gold it was, unless he was very much mistaken – a bit *too* solid, in fact, for he would have liked to take the whole thing away with him, and it was far too heavy to carry. Still, it was what was inside that really mattered – and that might be worth a fortune. What could it be?

Well, we shall soon know, thought the jackdaw. And with a slow, strong pull of his beak, he tugged away the lid and peered inside.

Even as he did so he uttered a muffled squawk of disappointment. A few withered flowers, and a sort of brown bean – that was all! His little green eyes were tinged with an angry red. All this fuss about nothing – it was a scandal, that was what it was! He felt as though Jill had been deliberately deceiving him, as though she had laid some elaborate plot to make him look a fool. It was enough to turn a respectable bird to crime!

A faint hope flickered in his heart. Perhaps the flowers were magic? Perhaps there was some special fragrance about them? He bent over the case and sniffed. No. There was nothing unusual. They just smelt sweet, that was all.

But wait a minute – didn't that bean *move*? Surely it had jumped, ever so slightly? If so, there must be something inside it. Aha! chuckled the jackdaw. Now we're getting somewhere! He snapped his beak together, several times, and then raised his head, prepared to strike at the chrysalis.

But no! Better wait. If there's anything alive inside the bean I might hurt it if I ripped it open. And it's sure to be worth more alive than dead. So I'll be careful with it. I'll take it in my beak and fly away with it, and give it to my beautiful witch. And she'll know what to do with it.

He bent down, took the chrysalis in his beak, opened his wings once more, and flew out into the night. High and fast against the wind he soared, out over the cruel cliffs, with the valley dreaming far below him, green and silver in the clouded moonlight. A dark shadow on a darker errand, an enemy of mankind, bearing as his prisoner a tiny creature who was powerless to fight against him.

Well, Mr Caterpillar had prayed that he might never be a butterfly. It would seem that at last his prayer had been answered, though not in the way that he would have desired.

14. What the Jackdaw Found

It was a sad little party that sat down to breakfast in the children's tent on the following morning. The turning of the caterpillar into a chrysalis would have been bad enough, but the total disappearance of the chrysalis itself was much worse.

'I suppose it really *was* Mr Caterpillar inside the chrysalis?' asked Jack.

'Of course it was,' answered Jill. 'Here's his letter to prove it.'

'Do you think he might have turned into a butterfly already and have flown off somewhere?' This suggestion came from the Imp.

Jill shook her head. 'I'm quite sure it couldn't be anything like that. It takes ages and ages for a chrysalis to turn into a butterfly.'

'It mightn't take so long up here on the Mountain,' rejoined the Imp. 'The air's full of all sorts of magic.'

'I know. That's why he was so anxious to come here. But even if he *had* turned into a butterfly, he certainly wouldn't have flown off like that without even saying goodbye.'

It was not only in the children's tent that the caterpillar – or rather, the chrysalis – was the main topic of conversation. He was also being discussed, with some heat, in the witch's cave.

'You wretched, stupid, black, wicked, nasty, ungrateful bird!' That was what the witch had cried when the jackdaw had proudly deposited the chrysalis on her breakfast table. 'I told you to get a compass and all you bring back is a horrid little bean.'

'It isn't a bean,' retorted the jackdaw in a very sulky voice. 'It's got something in it.'

'I don't care what it's got in it. It's completely worthless.'

'Then why did she keep it in a gold box?'

'Don't ask *me* why she keeps things in gold boxes. I don't know how that nasty child's mind works. What I *would* like to know is why you didn't steal the box itself. We could have done with a bit of gold.'

'It was too heavy,' muttered the jackdaw.

'That only makes it worse,' retorted the witch, somewhat unreasonably. 'If it was as heavy as that, it must have been worth a fortune. Whereas, *this* wretched thing's only fit to throw into the fire.'

With which she picked up the chrysalis between her skinny fingers and aimed it directly at the fire. For one breathless moment it seemed as though Mr Caterpillar's days were indeed ended; and then, just as she raised her arm, the jackdaw flew forward with an angry squawk, and seized the chrysalis in his beak. He was not going to let her destroy something which he had taken so much trouble to get.

'You rude, black, wretched thing!' screamed the witch. 'Give it back this instant!'

But the jackdaw was not going to give it back, and flew outside, carrying the chrysalis with him.

'Why d'you keep nagging him like that?' growled Sam. 'He'll fly off altogether one of these days.'

'Good riddance too,' snorted the witch. 'Such manners I never met before.'

'I don't care a hoot about his manners. He's useful.'

'What for?'

'Well, he's the only one who's come anywhere near finding the cave we want.'

The witch grunted with annoyance. It was all too true. The jackdaw *had* been useful, and on several occasions had led them to likely places.

So she stifled her anger, and went to the entrance.

'Mr Jackdaw! Mr Jackdaw!' she called in her sweetest voice. 'Please come in again! I won't say another word.'

The jackdaw, who was perched on the stump of a ruined tree, merely glanced at her with his little green eyes.

'*Please!*' entreated the witch. 'I promise I won't even touch your beautiful bean.'

The jackdaw still hesitated. But since he was really devoted to his evil mistress, in spite of her snappy ways, he finally fluttered back into the cave. And while her back was turned he cunningly pushed the chrysalis into a crack in the wood of the mantelpiece. It would be safe there, and he would be able to keep an eye on it from time to time, in case the thing inside ever showed any sign of coming out.

So maybe we have not seen the last of Mr Caterpillar after all.

*

For several days things went on much as usual, with both sides exploring – the children for the treasure which they really believed to exist, the witch and Sam for the great cave which they hoped would enable them to carry out their plans for the children's destruction.

And then, one day, the jackdaw came flying back to the cave in a state of great excitement.

'I've found it!' he squawked. 'I've found the very place!'

The jackdaw hesitated, but only for a moment, for he was really bursting with desire to tell them what he had found.

Briefly, it was this. You may remember that what Sam and the witch really wanted was a huge cave with a very narrow entrance – a cave that would be big enough to hold the whole population, and yet be so small at one end that it could be blocked in a few moments, so that everybody inside would be caught like rats in a trap.

This place, according to Mr Jackdaw, was ideal. Not only was it completely secluded, so that they could work without arousing comment, but it had a secret entrance which nobody would ever have suspected.

'Let's go and see it this very moment,' cried the witch, and Sam, for once in a way, agreed with her,

They had only been walking for five minutes, going downhill all the time, with the jackdaw flying in front of them, when the jackdaw wheeled sharply to the left, and flew into a small wood that seemed to be set against a solid wall of cliff. But no, for as they plunged into the wood they saw that there was a cleft in the rock, so narrow that they could only just scramble through. It was like a miniature mountain pass. It went on for about a hundred yards, and then, without any warning, it emerged into a wild and tangled dell, shaped like a huge basin, and entirely shut in by the surrounding cliffs, as though some giant had built it to hide himself from prying eyes.

The witch skipped up and down with delight. 'It couldn't be better.'

'You haven't seen anything yet,' rejoined the jackdaw. 'Follow me! And be careful not to tread too hard on the bracken. We don't want to leave any tracks.'

Obediently they followed him, taking a winding path which led straight to what seemed, once again, to be a solid block of rock.

'I can't see any way out of this,' muttered Sam.

'Perhaps you can't,' rejoined the witch, 'but that's no reason for scowling. Do try and enter *in* to things.' She felt so cross with him that she forgot where she was going, and almost entered into a puddle.

'Watch me!' cried the jackdaw.

They stood still and watched. He flew up to the rock, fluttered his wings, paused to peck at a big clump of ivy that crawled over the rock face, and then . . . hey presto . . . he had vanished.

*

Sam stared after him. 'He's gone!'

'He's gone!' echoed the witch.

From behind the ivy came the mocking laughter of the jackdaw.

'No I haven't. Come closer and you'll see!'

Walking very gingerly, to conceal their traces, they approached the rock. The witch gave a shrill scream. 'Look . . . it's hollow!'

'It's hollow all right,' came the muffled voice of the jackdaw. 'Come inside! But mind you don't tear the ivy!'

With great caution she parted the ivy, which hung over the hole like a thick curtain. Sam followed, grunting with excitement. For a few yards they had to crawl on their hands and knees, but then they could stand upright. They were in a long winding gallery, dimly lit by the sunlight that filtered through the ivy.

'It's the most wonderful entrance,' breathed the witch, 'but where does it lead?'

'That's the best part of it,' chuckled the jackdaw. 'You'll see in a minute.'

He flew down the corridor and they groped their way after him. Soon they were in almost pitch darkness, and then there was a sharp turn and the gallery opened into an immense cave, whose towering walls were bathed from top to bottom in a radiant, silver glow.

They stood there, silent, clutching the walls, staggered by the grandeur of the sight.

'It *is* a Treasure Trove!' gasped the witch.

'Don't be dumb,' retorted Sam, who knew more about these things. 'It's phosphorus.'

Which indeed it was – a huge, natural quarry of phosphorus, which, of course, shines in the dark.

'Though in a way you're right,' he added, 'for it would be worth a mint of money . . . if we could ever get it away.'

'Whatever it's worth,' rejoined the witch, 'it *looks* as if it's worth millions and millions. At any rate, that's what the animals will think. Oh, what a clever bird he is! Look! This part of the wall isn't solid at all.'

The jackdaw perched on her shoulder. 'No. That's the best thing about it. Because that's where we can build the tunnel. It goes right through to the outside.'

The witch clapped her hands with glee. 'I see the whole plan. We'll keep our own entrance a secret. And we'll start the animals digging on the other side, till they come right through. Then we'll walk in, as though we'd never been in here before, and tell them that nobody else must follow till we've made a thorough inspection. Then we'll come out again, and say that there's such a terrible lot of treasure that we must sort it out, and that everybody must parade on the following day . . . every single creature, so that there's nobody left outside at all. And then, when they're all here . . .'

She did not finish the sentence, but made a terrible grimace, and threw up her hands in the air, to imitate a huge explosion.

'Why can't we just let 'em all come in by the passage we've just used?' demanded Sam.

'For two reasons, silly. Firstly, because we want a separate exit by which we can escape ourselves. And secondly, because we want to be quite sure that *everybody's* inside. The only way to do that is by getting them all excited about digging the tunnel, working them up till they're half crazy. Besides . . .' and here she began to chuckle '. . . we want a little fun, don't we? And that's my idea of fun. Watching 'em all *digging their own graves!*'

Her chuckles grew louder and louder, and soon Sam joined in with his gruff guffaws, and the jackdaw with his shrill squawks. And there, for the moment, we must leave them, with the echoes of their unholy laughter ringing round the silver walls.

15. An Eagle Falls

Things began to move very quickly after the jackdaw's discovery of the cave. A return visit on the following morning convinced them that it was indeed the perfect place, without a single drawback. The witch even found the exact spot where, when the time came, she would place her charge of dynamite, and she was so pleased that her fingers itched to light it at that very moment.

'And now,' she said, 'we've got to tell those two brats, and after that we must call on Mr Eagle.'

'Why do we have to go climbing all that way to see that mouldy old bird?'

'Because he's the boss. Because what he says in these parts goes. We want them *all* digging, because we're not going to run the risk of leaving any witnesses behind. If he tells them to dig, they'll dig. And when he's heard what I've got to say, he *will* tell them to dig.'

So they set out to pay their calls, putting on their best clothes for the occasion.

The children were delighted to see them, and to hear their news. And any misgivings which the Imp might have had about the scheme were forgotten when he heard the witch enlarging on the riches which were in store for them all. If there was so much to be gained, surely the children would stay here for ages and ages? And surely he could banish his dread of being left alone?

'I *knew* my darling Sam would find it in the end,' proclaimed Miss Smith in a girlish voice, clasping her hands and gazing in the direction of Sam. 'Of course, it's all been a terrible strain on him. Night after night he's been sitting up over the cauldron, mixing powders and reciting magic spells till really I thought he'd be quite worn out. "Do stop it," I said to him over and over again, "and take a rest. What do a million rubies *matter*? What do we *want* with diamonds the size of footballs? And what can we *do* with all those rooms and rooms of gold? Do go to bed," I said to him, "and forget all about it." But no. He just went on and on. And at last . . . well, here we are!'

'How did he actually find it?' asked Jack.

'In a vision, my dear. Didn't you, Sam darling?'

'That's right,' growled Sam.

'A *beautiful* vision, wasn't it, my precious?'

Sam was feeling very foolish, and wished she would stop talking. Once again he grunted . . . 'That's right.'

'And it led us right to the very spot – the spot where we shall be leading *you* tomorrow, to help us dig for the treasure and share the reward!'

'How can you be so *sure* that the treasure's there?'

It was the Imp who spoke. He hated having to ask the question, but he felt that it was his duty. For though he was as anxious as any of them that there should be a treasure, he could not understand how Sam and the witch could just stand in front of a solid cliff, point at it, and say 'there's a treasure inside'.

His words caught Miss Smith unawares. But she rose to the occasion.

'Well really,' she said, pretending to look very offended,

'I *must* say I think that's a very peculiar question. After all, my husband . . .' and here she turned back to Sam '. . . my husband isn't exactly an *amateur* in these matters. He's found diamonds in India and gold in Australia and rubies in Spain and . . . and . . . and all sorts of things in all sorts of places. Haven't you, darling?'

Sam gave a smart twist to his wizard's cap. 'That's right,' he growled. 'I've found things everywhere.'

'So why you should suddenly assume that he doesn't know what he is talking about . . .'

'I wasn't assuming,' interrupted the Imp hastily, for Jill had cast a reproachful glance in his direction. 'I only wanted to be sure!'

'Well, you *can* be sure,' retorted the witch. 'I hope everybody *else* is sure?'

'*I'm* sure!' cried Jill. For it would almost have broken her heart to think that Miss Smith might be wrong.

'So am I!' echoed Jack, jumping with glee. 'As sure as sure!'

'That's right, my darling,' said the witch. 'And don't let anybody give you any silly ideas.' Here she tossed her head scornfully at the Imp. 'We shall need your help when we start to dig tomorrow. In fact we shall need everybody's help, which is why I'm off to see Mr Eagle this very minute. Sam darling . . . we must take our leave.'

With much waving of hands and blowing of kisses, she started up the cliff path, followed by Sam, who held tightly to his wizard's cap, leaving the children eagerly discussing their plans for the following day.

*

Mr Eagle was keeping watch in his eyrie when Sam and the witch set out to visit him, and since he had eagle eyes – even eaglier than most eagles – he saw them when they were still a very long way off, and guessed that they were on their way to the Eagle Estate Agency. So he quickly spread his wings and swooped down to the hut in order to be ready to receive them.

Finally Miss Smith and Sam entered and seated themselves in front of Mr Eagle's perch, in order to explain their business. As usual, Miss Smith did all the talking. And she was so carried away by her own enthusiasm that at first she did not realize that Mr Eagle was not paying much attention.

It was therefore with something of a shock that she noticed that he was actually stifling a yawn.

She sat up very sharply. 'I hope you understand what I am telling you, Mr Eagle?' she demanded.

'Perfectly, madam, perfectly,' responded Mr Eagle, in polite but weary tones. 'Rubies, diamonds, emeralds. Most interesting. Pray continue!'

He closed his eyes and clasped his claws in front of him, looking like a very old judge who has to listen to a very dull case in a court of law. To tell the truth, he *was* rather bored by the whole business, and for a very good reason; he could not see what there could possibly be in it for *him*. If it had been *his* Treasure Trove, that would have been quite different; he would have been able to fly here, there and everywhere, issuing orders and bossing people about, and that would have been very agreeable. But as it was not his Trove, it was quite obvious that these two wretched Humans would be doing all the bossing, and that was an idea he simply could not abide.

But he had even stronger objections, though he did not mention them. If every inhabitant of the Mountain were suddenly turned into a millionaire, what would happen to his authority? Supposing, for example, that Mr Crow were to turn up at the office with a diamond tiara perched on the top of his head, how would it be possible to treat him as though he were just an ordinary, penniless clerk? If Mrs Rabbit was going to line the floor of the rabbit warren with rubies, it was quite certain that she would very quickly get ideas far above her station. It is true that Mr Eagle had no very clear notion of what rubies actually were, but everybody always spoke of them as though they were extremely important and delicious, and he did not like the idea of such a lot of important and delicious things going to such unsuitable people. It was anarchy. That was what it was – anarchy and revolution, and he would have no part in it.

The witch with her uncanny instinct began to guess his thoughts. 'Oh, ho!' she muttered to herself. 'So *that's* how it is! The old bird thinks he'll be knocked off his perch! And he will . . . he will! But we mustn't let him suspect that . . . not yet.'

She leant forward, and over her face there spread a look of great cunning.

'Mr Eagle,' she said, in a soft persuasive voice, 'we haven't yet mentioned the best thing of all that we shall be able to get out of the Trove.'

'Indeed? And what is that?'

'There is a great deal of gold in the Treasure Trove.'

'So I understand,' he replied, with little enthusiasm.

'Ah, yes. But what can we *make* with the gold?'

Mr Eagle stifled another yawn. 'I have no idea. A number of useful objects, no doubt.'

'There is one object in particular that might be very useful indeed.'

'Such as?'

'A crown!'

Mr Eagle sat up with a jerk. For the first time he was interested. 'Do you think we could really make a crown?'

There was a moment's awkward pause. Then, as though she were about to divulge some extra-special secret, she whispered: 'Of course, there is *one* crown we should have to make.'

Mr Eagle's heart began to thump with excitement, because he guessed that she meant a crown for him. However, he pretended not to understand.

'Indeed, madam? And which crown is that?'

'Oh, Mr Eagle! Surely you can guess?'

Mr Eagle shook his head.

'Who is the one great figure on the Mountain who was obviously born to wear a crown?'

Mr Eagle's heart thumped faster and faster, for he was now quite certain that she was referring to himself. But he still pretended not to understand.

'The one great figure on the Mountain?' he repeated. 'Who could that be?' He bent his head and peered out through the narrow window, as though in search of this unknown person. But there was nobody in sight but Mrs Rabbit, who was nibbling dandelions in the shadow of a distant hedge. So he turned again to Miss Smith and said, 'You mystify me, madam!'

'Oh, Mr Eagle, how can you be so . . . so modest? Why, the crown would be for yourself, of course!'

Mr Eagle gave a deep sigh of satisfaction. So he had been right!

'For me? Surely not?'

'But yes, Mr Eagle. It would be only right and proper. Wouldn't it, Sam darling?'

'Very proper indeed,' replied Sam. 'Just the thing.'

'I've often thought how splendid you'd look in a crown,' continued the witch. 'Haven't I, Sam?'

'You have indeed,' he lied.

'Not just a little crown, of course.'

'Oh, no!' agreed Sam. 'A very big crown.'

Mr Eagle was in the seventh heaven. If they were really going to provide him with a crown, and if nobody else was to be allowed to have one, then his whole feeling about the Treasure Trove would be completely altered. He would do his utmost to help them with the scheme.

The witch perceived that her work was done.

'Well,' she said, rising to her feet, 'we must not delay you any longer. And we may count on your support?'

'In every way, madam,' he replied. 'I will issue the necessary orders at once.'

'In that case, if you will excuse us . . .'

She finished the sentence by sweeping a low curtsey. And then they both walked out backwards, as though they were indeed in the presence of a king.

For a few moments Mr Eagle remained swaying on his perch, his eyes closed, conjuring up all sorts of delightful visions of the future, in which he was always the central figure, with a large crown on his head. He wondered how soon it would be ready and when would be the first occasion that he would wear it. He even wondered if perhaps he could arrange that there should be some sort of coronation. A coronation! The thought made him feel so dizzy that he had to clutch at his perch.

16. Discord in the Dell

'If they keep working as hard as this we'll be right through the tunnel by the end of the week!'

So spoke Miss Smith, chuckling with glee as she watched the busy scene before her. It was nearing the end of the third day of the Great Digging, and the little dell was so crowded with animals that sometimes it was quite difficult to move. The air was thick with dust as they hurried backwards and forwards with stones and sticks and clods of earth, and there was such a sound of squeaking and chattering and purring and buzzing that one had to raise one's voice to be heard at all.

Yes, Mr Eagle had certainly been as good as his word. Within an hour of the witch's visit he had issued his orders, which were as short and clear as a call to battle. Every inhabitant of the Mountain *must* parade at dawn at the entrance to the dell in order to take part in the Great Digging. It was as simple as that. There were to be no exceptions whatsoever.

'What about Mr Sloth?' the Imp had asked, when Mr Eagle had handed him the first batch of notices to stick up on trees and push down burrows. 'It'll take a lot to move *him*.'

'I am glad you mentioned Mr Sloth,' returned Mr Eagle, in severe tones. 'I have a very poor regard for Mr Sloth, hanging upside down on a tree for weeks at a time, doing absolutely nothing. This will be a good opportunity for him to mend his ways. You had better leave a special notice on Mr Sloth. And to make quite certain that he sees it you can fasten it to him with a pin.'

'Supposing I stick the pin in a little too far?' asked the Imp, with a twinkle in his eye.

'In the circumstances I think you would be quite justified in doing so.'

So poor Mr Sloth, having been sharply pricked with a pin, was there with the rest of them, doing more work than he had ever done in his life, and absolutely hating it.

But Mr Sloth was an exception. The vast majority of the animals were thoroughly enjoying themselves.

Never in the whole course of her life had Mrs Rabbit enjoyed herself so much. She and Mr Rabbit and all the little rabbits were always among the first arrivals at the cliff, and as soon as they got there they set to work with a will, and all you could see of them was a row of little white tails, bobbing up and down, as they burrowed deeper and deeper into the earth. Burrowing was the one accomplishment in which Mrs Rabbit felt definitely superior to Mrs Hare; and she never failed to thrill with delight when she saw that haughty creature trying, in vain, to keep pace with her. She would pause in her work, and bob over to see how she was doing.

'Dear me!' she would say, staring with wide eyes at the very small hole which Mrs Hare had managed to dig. 'Have you just started a *new* hole today?'

She knew quite well that it was the same hole that Mrs Hare had been digging all yesterday, which made the question all the more irritating.

'I really could not say,' replied Mrs Hare, in an off-hand

manner. 'One digs where one feels inclined.'

'Well, one has certainly chosen a nice soft place,' rejoined Mrs Rabbit. 'I expect one will be right through to the other side in a few minutes.'

Mrs Hare did not deign to reply to this remark, but turned her back on Mrs Rabbit, and put all her strength into her burrowing, while Mrs Rabbit sat calmly down and watched her.

'Perhaps,' said Mrs Rabbit at length, 'you would like a little help?'

'Not at all,' gasped Mrs Hare, who was already out of breath. 'I seem to have come up against a rock.'

'A rock?' Mrs Rabbit pushed her nose into the entrance. And before Mrs Hare could stop her she had plunged inside, and out of the hole shot a positive stream of dirt and pebbles which almost hit Mrs Hare in the face. Then she emerged again, quite composed and without even a speck of dirt on her nose.

'No rocks at all,' she said. 'Very easy going. I expect you will be ahead of us all in no time.'

To which Mrs Hare only responded with an icy look; and then she walked stiffly back into the hole.

*

Among the best workers were the zebra family. Complaining, as they did, of the cold, they welcomed this opportunity of exercise, and were never still for a moment, sweeping away piles of rubble with their hooves, or seizing clods of earth between their strong white teeth. The very sight of them made Mr and Mrs Polar-Bear feel quite faint, for, as you may remember, *they* had come down from the higher regions, and were always complaining of the *heat*.

Mrs Polar-Bear, looking quite exhausted, would wander up to a heap of stones, with the intention of carrying off an armful of them to the dump, and then, the very thought of such exertion would be too much for her, and she would recline heavily on them, and fan herself with anything that came handy.

'Really,' she would say, in a faint voice, 'how these creatures manage it in this heat I simply cannot imagine. I, for one, am stifled.'

Mr Polar-Bear would then sink by her side. 'It was your idea to come,' he snapped.

'One must do one's duty,' she retorted. 'One cannot idle when there is work to be done.' To prove that she was not idling she picked up a very small pebble in a very languid paw and tossed it in the direction of the dump. However, her aim was so feeble that it only landed on the nose of Mrs Zebra, who gave a loud whinny of disapproval.

Needless to say, Mr and Mrs George Goat were there, though sometimes the other animals wished they would stay away, for Mr Goat was really more trouble than he was worth; his one idea of helping was to take a running jump at anything in his path and give it a powerful butt with his head.

'Poor George . . . such a *fool*,' said his wife, over and over again. 'Look at him *now*!'

Sure enough there was George, charging head-first at a big log which Mr and Mrs Beaver had painfully carried to the top of the slope. Crash went his head and down rolled the log, so that the beavers had to carry it all the way back again. However, they did not really mind, for they enjoyed the work more than they could have told you. 'Next to building a dam,' Mrs Beaver would observe, 'this is really the pleasantest way in which one could possibly pass the time.'

And over them all, perched on a high tree, following the work with an ever-watchful eye, was Mr Eagle. If the truth had been known, he was longing to fly off his perch and join them; however, that would have been beneath his dignity, so he confined himself to issuing instructions through Mr Crow, who sat on a smaller branch some feet below him, armed with a notebook.

Thus Mr Eagle would say: 'Mr Goat has no *method*. None at all. He is all butt and no brain. Make a note of it, Mr Crow.'

And Mr Crow would pretend to make a note of it,

though of course all he did was to open his notebook and give it a sharp peck.

And the children? Well, you can imagine how they were enjoying themselves! Jack, being the only one with a spade, was kept busy all day long, and Jill was running here, there and everywhere on a thousand errands. Some of those errands, one must admit, were very comical, because many of the animals were so small or so simple that they were not really very much use. However, Jill encouraged them all to believe that they were of the utmost importance – even the tiny Dormouse family, whom she found huddled together, looking very lost and bewildered, in the shadow of a big rock. Poor little dormice! They were longing to join in the fun, but what could they do with all those great sticks and stones? So Jill set them to work on moving a small heap of straw which was piled a few yards away. There was no real reason to move it, and she herself could have lifted it up in a moment and taken it wherever she wanted. But it made the dormice feel very happy to be given this work, and they trotted backwards and forwards with a will, carrying straws in their mouths as if the whole treasure depended on their exertions.

*

The only person who was not really happy was the Imp. Try as he would, he could not rid himself of these feelings of fear and foreboding. The last thing he wanted to be was a spoil-sport, and yet . . . his sharp little eyes were constantly noticing details which escaped the others, details which disturbed and alarmed him.

For instance, why did the jackdaw always stay perched so firmly on the ledge of rock that jutted out a few yards to the left of the tunnel? There was a big cluster of ivy just below this rock, and whenever any of the animals came too near to it, he flew at them, swearing and pecking, and squawking at them to go away. Why? Could he be concealing something? But what? As far as he could see, it was only a bush of ivy rooted in the cliff. What possible reason could the jackdaw have for keeping them away from *that*?

And then there was the behaviour of Mrs Smith – for that, of course, was the name by which he knew the witch. Whenever he approached her, she always stopped talking to Sam, and quickly changed the conversation, as though she were afraid of his overhearing what she had been saying. And yet, from time to time he *did* overhear a few words . . . words which sent a cold shiver down his spine, even though he did not fully understand them.

Only a few hours ago, for instance, he had come upon her unawares, when she was talking to Sam, and he had seen her point towards the children and had heard her say: 'Well, one thing we can be sure of is that those two brats will never grow old!' He had pretended not to hear what she had said, but he could not help noticing that she went pale with anger when she saw him standing nearby. And afterwards, when he was alone again, he sat down and tried to work out what this strange sentence could have signified. That word 'brats' . . . he seemed to have heard it somewhere else, long, long ago, in a different world, and though he could not have told you exactly what it meant, he was quite certain that it was not a kindly word; it was not a word you would use about children if you really had love for them in your heart. Then again . . . 'they will never grow old'? Of course, it *might* have meant nothing at all – she might just have been saying that they were so full of high spirits that one could never imagine them growing up. And yet . . . another meaning was possible, a meaning so dark and terrible that he hardly dared to think about it.

And yet he must think about it. Not only that, he must *do* something about it. But what?

He decided on the bravest course of all. He would go up to Jill and tell her what he feared. It might cost him her friendship, but he loved her so dearly that he must risk even that.

With head held high, he walked towards her.

*

Forced with the need to put his forebodings into words, the Imp felt at a loss. How could he explain to Jill all the tiny signs and signals which seemed to him to point to danger?

'I'm worried,' he stammered at length. 'About the treasure. Supposing we find there isn't any at all?'

Jill stared at him in astonishment. 'It's rather late in the day to say that, isn't it?'

'Perhaps it is. But I . . . I don't trust the Smiths.'

Jill's face clouded. It was not the first time that the Imp had spoken unkindly of the Smiths behind their backs, and she did not like it. 'It's also rather late in the day to say that,' she replied coldly. 'Why don't you trust them?'

The Imp could have given her a hundred reasons. He could have pointed to their friendship with the jackdaw, he could have quoted Miss Smith's strange love of the skeleton – for the Imp was one of the few people who had ever seen it – he could even have mentioned the little puffs of green smoke which on more than one occasion he had seen coming out of her nostrils. However, all these things seemed unconvincing. So he said:

'It was something I saw just now.'

'What did you see?'

'I saw her point at you and Jack and I heard her say something.'

'What did she say?'

'That you would never grow old.' Even as he quoted her words the Imp realized how innocent they sounded when he repeated them. When *she* had spoken it was different . . . for she had spoken with a hiss and a twist of the lip; she had put hatred into them. But how could he explain that to Jill? The Imp could not hiss and when his lips twisted it was only to smile.

Jill laughed in his face. 'Well, really,' she exclaimed, 'I must say that I can't see anything very wrong in that.'

'It might mean . . .'

'What?'

The Imp did not dare to say aloud what it might mean, it was too terrible.

So feebly he muttered . . . 'Anything.'

Jill stared at him in bewilderment. What was the matter with him? Why did he come and bother her like this, when she was so busy, and try to fill her with all sorts of unpleasant feelings? That was not how a good friend ought to behave; and for the first time in her life she found herself wondering if he really *was* such a good friend after all.

Then suddenly she bethought herself of the magic compass. It was in her bag at that very moment; why had not she remembered it before? She had only to look at it and all her doubts would be solved. By pointing it directly at the tunnel she would be able to tell at once whether happiness or danger lay at the other end of it. Even more important, by pointing it directly at the Imp she would be able to tell whether he was a friend or a foe. Not that she really doubted him; she was convinced of his affection for her, in spite of the fact that he was being so very tiresome at the moment; it was just that she wanted to be quite, quite sure.

However, she must not let him see what she was doing.

'Will you excuse me for a minute?' she said. 'There seems to be some trouble at the entrance to the tunnel, and I had better go over to see what it is.'

Now near the entrance to the tunnel, as you may remember, the jackdaw was stationed, keeping guard over the other entrance, which nobody knew was there. And when he saw Jill draw near, and take out the compass from her bag, he chortled to himself. For only the night before he had stolen it from the tent for the second time, and returned it after the witch had made quite certain that it was in order – or rather, that it was *not* in order, but wickedly changed to suit her convenience. So he knew that however she turned or twisted it, she would never learn the truth.

He watched her closely through his little green eyes. He saw her point it directly at the entrance to the tunnel, and as she bent down to see what it said, he noticed a little smile of contentment spread over her face. Good!

That meant that the needle had swung round to PEACE and HAPPINESS. If she only knew! The jackdaw began to shake with silent laughter.

And now, where was she going to turn it? Perhaps she would turn it at him? So much the better if she did; it would have amused him to be given a good character for once in a while. But no – she was turning the other way. And now she was pointing it directly at the Imp.

The jackdaw leant forward to see how she was reacting. At first he could not see her face, for she was bending over the compass a second time, as though she could not believe the evidence before her. Then she raised her head again, and this time there could be no mistake about what she was feeling. She had turned very pale, her lips were set in a grim line, and she was staring in the direction of the Imp with a look of anger and dismay.

For a moment she stayed there quite still. Then she pushed the compass back in her bag, tossed her head, and walked swiftly over to the Imp. The jackdaw could not hear what she was saying, but it must have been something very unpleasant indeed. For he saw the Imp turn very red, and look very angry – he saw him trying to speak, without success, for Jill held up her hand to stop him – and then he saw her turn sharply away, and go off to speak to her brother. The Imp made as if to follow, but then he too turned away, and strode to the entrance of the dell. For the last time he turned round, staring in Jill's direction. Then he brushed aside the branches that overhung the exit, and vanished from the scene.

17. The Imp in the Dark

The hours went by, the sun rose in the heavens and sank again, the day's work ended in the dell, and the animals all trooped home to their burrows and their caves and their nests, tired but happy.

'Only two days more!' the witch had cried to them, over and over again, as she stood at the entrance, bidding them good night.

'Two days more and the treasure will be yours!' Sam had grunted as he stood by her side.

'Two days . . . two days!' had squawked the jackdaw, beating the air with ragged wings.

The children were the last to take their leave.

'Tired, my dears?' the witch had asked, leaning close to Jill's pale face.

'A little,' sighed Jill.

'You mustn't overdo it,' warned the witch. 'It would be too terrible if you weren't both here on the great day.' And indeed it would have been, from the witch's point of view, for it would have wrecked all her plans.

'There's no danger of that,' returned Jill, forcing a smile. 'We shall be here.'

It was no ordinary fatigue that made Jill's cheeks so pale as the children wandered home; it was the result of her quarrel with the Imp. She had said the most dreadful things to him. She had told him that she did not trust him, that she did not believe in his friendship, and that she never wished to see him again.

On the evidence of the compass, what else *could* she have said to him?

And yet, it had hurt her most painfully to have to say such things. She felt that she could never forget the look of anguish that had passed over the Imp's face while she was upbraiding him – a look that had changed to one of fierce anger, as though she were accusing him unjustly – as though it were *she* who were to blame. But how could she be to blame? She was merely following the guidance of the compass, and that, she knew, could never lie.

Oh, well, it was all most unfortunate, and it was a miserable shame that it had ever happened, but there was no use brooding over it now. The best thing was to try to forget it by working all the harder. And then, when they had collected their share of the treasure, to pack up and make their way back home.

For the first time Jill felt that she really would not be sorry when this strange holiday was over.

*

And the Imp?

Perhaps we ought not to let you see him, at this moment, for his face was buried in his hands, and his shoulders were heaving, and he was sobbing and sobbing as though he could never stop.

During these past weeks he had dreamed of only one thing – the day when he would say goodbye to the Mountain for ever and join the children on the journey home. He had really no right to indulge in such a dream; he had received no permission from the Mountain, nor had the children even asked him to accompany them. But his heart was set on the scheme so passionately that he brushed aside all doubts. It would be winter when they went — so he told himself — and the Mountain would be fast asleep. As for the children not wanting him to come, how could that be, when they were always so friendly, when they had made him one of themselves?

But now, in the space of a few cruel minutes, all those dreams had been shattered. Jill had told him that she never wanted to see him again, never as long as she lived. It was the end of all his hopes.

Never, now, would he climb on to that cart and set off with them, down into the valley, over the hills and far away. Never would they trundle along, laughing and talking, while the great outlines of the Mountain slowly faded behind them, and a new world crept into view . . . a world which, though it was so new, would yet be strangely familiar, *his* world, the world where he belonged.

That was the heart of the Imp's grief; he knew that the Mountain was not his real home, he knew that somewhere another home was waiting for him, a home which he had lost a long, long time ago. How he had lost it, or where it was, he could not have told you; he just knew that it was somewhere in the great beyond. And ever since the children had come to the Mountain, he had been constantly reminded of that home; when they had lit the lamp in their tent he had seemed to see, in the back of his mind, another lamp that somebody, somewhere, had once lit for him. When they had cooked their evening meal over a fire of logs, he had sniffed the savour that floated up from the saucepan, and it had recalled to him, as from a great distance, another savour in some dim, forgotten kitchen where he had toddled as a baby. And when Jill had been near him, with her golden hair, he had remembered another lovely face that had once bent over him, when he was lying in his cradle.

But where did all these memories come from? To whom did he belong? Where was his real home? Who *was* he?

These were the questions he had hoped to answer. They

would never be answered now. He would stay on the Mountain alone. He would grow old among the animals. And when he died the animals might be sorry for him, but they would just push him into a burrow and cover him with leaves, and that would be that.

Which was why the Imp was weeping. You must admit, if you are a little boy or a little girl, that there have been times when you have wept for less than that.

But there is an end to all things, even to tears, and at length the Imp sniffed his last sniff, and wiped his cheeks for the last time, and straightened himself, and smoothed his hair, and stood up, prepared to go home to bed.

And then he paused, and folded his arms, and stared at the ground, deep in thought.

Why should he give up so easily? Why should he throw in the sponge, just because Jill had spoken to him so cruelly? There was some mystery there, now he came to think of it; it was incredible that she should suddenly have changed, so completely . . . at one moment a friend, at the next an enemy.

No. He would not give in. He would fight.

But how?

He made a great decision.

He would go back, at this very moment, to the dell, and search and search, till somehow he got to the bottom of the mystery. If he must, he would plunge into the tunnel, and tear away at the earth and the rocks till he got to the other side. He did not care what he did or what might happen; he was desperate; if the worst came to the worst he would go to Mrs Smith's cave and challenge her face to face.

His mind was made up. Nothing would stop him now. There was no time to waste, for the sun was almost set. As he strode down the hill, it shone on his face, and it seemed to light it to a smile.

*

The light was fast fading when the Imp crept through the cleft in the rock which led to the Treasure Trove, and he had to step warily lest he should trip in the shadows. But there was one shadow that he did not notice. For no sooner was he inside the dell, and tiptoeing across to the entrance to the Trove, than the jackdaw, who was on sentry duty in the dark branches of a neighbouring tree, floated silently above him, and vanished out of sight. The wicked bird, needless to say, was off to warn the witch of the Imp's arrival.

However, the Imp had no idea that he had been observed. He paused to look around him. How sad and desolate it all seemed! And how ugly! Wherever his eye rested there were piles of earth and pools of mud and heaps of pebbles; all the shrubs and flowering bushes had been trampled to death; it looked as though a battle had been raging. Yes, he said to himself, it was an evil day when the Smiths had come to the Mountain, and bitterly he reproached himself for not having taken earlier action against them. He wondered if, even now, it was too late – if he ought not perhaps to make a supreme effort, and set out on an all-night climb to the crater of the Mountain, and take the great risk of waking Him and asking His advice. But he shuddered at the very thought of it; supposing he were wrong, the Mountain's wrath would be so terrible that it might well destroy him. And there was a chance that he *might* be wrong. His suspicions and forebodings might be only the result of jealousy.

Well, there was only one way to find out, and that was to explore for himself. So he stepped right up to the entrance to the Trove.

Then he paused and stood very still, with his head cocked sharply to the left. At that moment there had come a puff of wind, which for a second had blown away a branch of the ivy that lay over the secret entrance. Through this tiny chink came a faint ray of light, which was, in fact, the reflection on the walls of the tunnel of the glow of phosphorus far within. In the broad daylight it would not have been noticeable, and even at this twilight hour it is doubtful whether you or I would have detected it; but the Imp had eyes of super-sharpness, and instantly guessed that he had stumbled on something of importance. Creeping softly up to the ivy – for he did not know what might lie behind it – he stretched out his hand to draw it aside.

And then . . .

'Good evening!'

It was the voice of the witch, like the hiss of a snake, only a few feet behind him.

He paused, rigid, trying to think. Even if he had wanted, there would have been no point in trying to escape. He would have no chance against creatures like Sam and the witch. But he did not want to escape. This was the show-down; he must stay on his ground and fight. Maybe, with any luck, he would be able to bluff it out.

He turned to face her.

'Good evening,' he replied.

If he had ever had any doubts about the wickedness of Miss Smith, they were gone for ever now. As she stepped forward in the half light, with the crescent moon behind her, she looked the very spirit of evil. Her face was contorted into a mask of rage, and green smoke poured from her nostrils as though she had been a human bonfire. As for Sam, who stood immediately behind her, he looked almost as horrifying. for his eyes were red with hatred and his teeth were bared like a wolf's when it sees its prey.

*

'A pleasant evening,' hissed the witch, in a strangled voice.

'Very pleasant,' echoed the Imp, trying to stop his knees from trembling.

'Having a look around?' snarled Sam, taking a step forward.

The witch restrained him with a skinny finger. 'Not just for a moment, darling,' she said. 'Perhaps we were mistaken.'

'Mistaken in what?' asked the Imp.

'In your intentions.'

The next half-hour was like a nightmare

'I had no intentions. I was merely – interested.'

'A darned sight too interested for our liking.' Sam came so close to him that the Imp could feel his hot breath on his cheek.

'Yes,' echoed the witch. 'Little boys should not be too inquisitive. It's apt to be dangerous.'

'For whom?' challenged the Imp. 'For me – or for you?'

They were the last words he was to speak for a very long time. For at that moment Sam threw himself on the Imp like a wild beast. The assault was so fierce and so unexpected that it was as though the whole Mountain had suddenly fallen on top of him. He staggered backwards, with a blinding pain in one eye, and an even fiercer pain in his stomach. And as he fell, he was conscious of two thick sweaty hands gripping his neck.

He tried to struggle out of reach, but what chance had he? A little boy against a grown man thrice his weight? He tried to cry out, but the hands were strangling his throat. And the pain . . . the pain.

'Gently . . . gently!' It was the witch's voice, and it seemed to come from a long distance.

'Let's kill him now . . . let's get rid of him for ever.'

'No, no. Gently, I tell you. He may still come in useful.'

Snarling and growling Sam loosened his hands. At the same time he tore the scarf from his neck and wrapped it tightly round the Imp's mouth, so that he could scarcely breathe. A moment later his hands and feet were bound with strong cords. And then they proceeded to drag him away.

The next half-hour was like a nightmare. He had a vague memory of being tugged down winding paths, with the sharp stones cutting his back and the thorny bushes scratching his face. From time to time, too, he shuddered with an extra pain, as Sam gave his arm a vicious twist, or kicked his legs with his sharp boots. Once he tried to open his eyes, but as soon as he did so, the jackdaw swooped above him, with threatening wings and a sharp beak, as though he were intent on blinding him. So he closed them again, screwing them up tightly, not only to save himself from the jackdaw, but to prevent the scalding tears from running down his cheeks.

'Gently . . . gently. We may need him yet.'

It was the witch's voice, once again. And as she spoke, he knew that they were dragging him into their cave.

'Are the ropes quite tight?' she demanded.

'Couldn't be tighter.' They were, indeed, cutting into his flesh.

'Then put him in this corner.'

He was hurled across the floor like a sack of potatoes. So fierce was his pain, and so exhausted was he by his struggles, that as his head hit the wall he fell into a dead faint.

And there, for the moment, we must leave him.

18. In the Witch's Cave

The long night dragged its weary length, and it was not till the first pale fingers of dawn crept through the witch's cave that the Imp began to recover consciousness. And even then, he was still so stunned and weak that he hardly knew where he was or what had happened. He was aware that two black shadows were hovering over him, and he felt a glass of water pressed to his lips, and he heard a hissing voice whisper . . . 'We'll keep him alive till we know what to do with him.' That was all. As soon as they had gone, the darkness seemed to close over him again.

Outside, had he only known it, events were marching to a swift and terrible climax. The scene in the dell, by the Treasure Trove, was one of the greatest bustle and confusion, for the end of the tunnel had almost been reached; only a few inches separated the crowd of animals from the great cave of phosphorus in which, on the following day, the witch was planning to destroy them.

Indeed, already a few cracks were gaping in the thin wall, and through these chinks came gleams of silver light, of such startling radiance that the animals were driven almost to a frenzy, for they felt that all the treasures of the universe were awaiting them within. At one moment it looked as though they could no longer be held in check; Sam had to throw himself bodily across the entrance, with arms outstretched, to prevent them from making a massed charge; and it needed all Mr Eagle's powers of persuasion to drive them back.

'Order! Order!' he had to cry, time and again, swooping over them with his great wings. 'Order! Order! ORDER!'

At last order was restored, and as the sun was setting, he fluttered up on to the topmost branch of the old oak that hung over the entrance to the Trove, and issued his commands for the following day. Everybody was to parade at nine o'clock in the morning. They were to line up at the entrance, and to march in in single file. Nobody was to touch anything till he gave the official signal. And finally, they were to observe strict alphabetical order.

'Absolutely ridiculous!' snapped Mrs Hare, when she heard this last condition. 'If we are to keep in strict alphabetical order it will mean that all the ants will have to lead the way. And really . . . the idea of walking behind the ants . . .'

She felt so indignant, that she could not even finish the sentence.

A great many other animals were also feeling indignant. It looked like being a stormy meeting on the morrow.

*

That night, in their tent, the children discussed their plans for the following day.

'How much treasure do you think we ought to take?' asked Jill.

'Well, Sam said that we could take as much as ever we wanted. So why don't we drive down in the cart, and load it up?'

Jill shook her head. 'I think that would look terribly

141

greedy,' she said. 'It isn't as if anybody else had a cart.'

'Perhaps it would,' agreed Jack. 'Supposing we each took a big basket?'

'That would look much better. Then we could fill one basket with gold, and the other with diamonds.'

Jack clapped his hands with glee. 'And rubies and emeralds and sapphires!' he cried. 'Oh Jill, won't it be fun? Just think of what Mummy will say when she sees them!'

Jill smiled. 'Or of what Daddy will say when he sees all that gold!'

'We shall be able to keep some of it, shan't we?'

'Of course we shall.'

'Just think of what we shall be able to buy!'

For a little while the children gave themselves up to dreaming of all the wonderful riches which were so nearly theirs.

Then Jack gave a long sigh. 'There's only one thing I'm sorry about,' he said.

'What's that?'

'I do wish we hadn't quarrelled with the Imp.'

Jill frowned. 'So do I. But it's too late to worry about that now.'

'Don't you think we could possibly make it up?'

'How could we? You know what the compass said.'

'You're sure you read it right?'

'Of course I'm sure.'

'You don't think Grannie could have made a mistake?'

'Oh, Jack, when did Grannie ever make a mistake?'

Jack shook his head in bewilderment. 'I just can't understand it. He seemed so nice. And he seemed to like us so much. He seemed to like *you* most of all.'

Jill was glad that the light was so dim, for otherwise her brother would have seen that she was blushing. Yes – it was only too true that the Imp had seemed to like her very much indeed. That only made it worse.

'D'you know what I'd hoped?' asked Jack. 'I'd hoped that when we went home the Imp might have come with us.'

Jill nodded. She too, in her secret heart, had hoped just the same thing.

'I don't believe he really belongs here. Oh, yes . . . I know that he's always lived with the animals, and that he's never been to school, and that he's not a bit like anybody else we've met. All the same, I do feel that he *wants* to be just like an ordinary boy . . . now that he's met you and me. It's almost as though he had been lost, for years and years, and had suddenly found himself . . .'

'Please don't go on,' interrupted Jill, who was very near to tears. 'It only makes me feel miserable. I want to forget all about him.'

'All right,' returned Jack. 'I won't say any more. In any case, I don't suppose we shall ever see him again.'

With which he curled himself up in his blanket and was soon asleep.

Sleep came less easily to Jill. And when at last she dozed off, it was only to dream of the Imp. They were not happy dreams, for she fancied that he was lost in a dark forest, and was calling her name, as though she alone could save him.

*

Had Jill known the true state of the Imp's fortunes that night, her heart would have been even more sorely troubled.

For Sam and the witch were also discussing their plans for the morrow, and among them was a plan to take his life.

By this time he had regained consciousness, and though he was still faint from pain and hunger – for all they had given him to eat was a crust of dry bread, washed down with a cup of dirty water – he was able to follow what they were saying. And as the full horror of their schemes gradually dawned upon him, his blood ran cold.

The witch, with the jackdaw perched on her shoulder, was standing at the entrance to the cave, sniffing the night air and scanning the moonlit sky.

'It'll be fine and clear when morning comes,' she said, in

a gloating voice. 'That's how we want it . . . fine and clear. They'll all be there, every one of 'em.'

'What time d'you reckon they'll be through the tunnel?' asked Sam.

'About noon.'

'You'd better make it noon *sharp*,' he grunted. 'We don't want to run any risks. As soon as they're all inside the big cave they'll start yelling for the treasure, and if any of 'em were to suspect that there wasn't any treasure at all, they might turn nasty.'

'That's true enough,' agreed the witch. 'We'll make it noon sharp.'

'OK. At exactly that moment I'll block the main entrance, run down the tunnel into the cave, say a word to that old eagle telling him to keep everybody quiet for a few minutes, and then we'll do a bolt through our secret exit.'

'And what about *me?*' squawked the jackdaw.

'What about my precious?' crooned the witch, stroking his wicked head. 'Why, you'll be perched on Mummy's shoulder all the time. And when we're safely outside you can watch me strike the match which will light the fuse to the dynamite.'

Dynamite! When the Imp heard this terrible word it was as much as he could do to prevent himself from crying out loud. The whole hideous plan revealed itself in a single flash. He felt as though he were looking into the very jaws of death, and he could not move a finger to escape.

'What about *him?*' grunted Sam.

As he spoke he jerked his thumb towards the Imp, who quickly closed his eyes, feigning unconsciousness.

'Well, what *about* him?' retorted the witch.

'Oughtn't he to be blown up with all the others?'

The witch laughed scornfully. 'Oh, yes!' she jeered. 'That's a *wonderful* idea! We'll carry him into the cave, gagged and bound, and let everybody see what's been happening. And *won't* they all be pleased!'

'There's no need to get sarcastic,' snarled Sam.

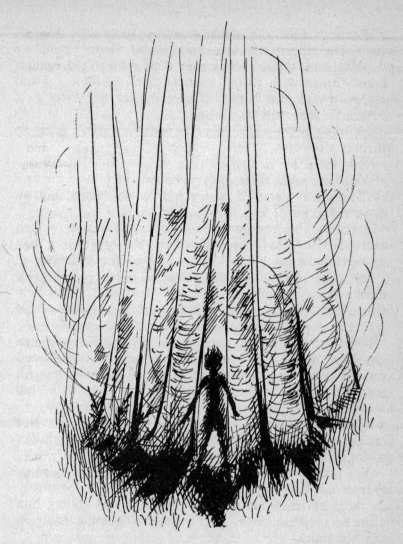

She fancied that he was lost in a dark forest

'How can I help it when you say such silly things?'
The witch tapped her foot impatiently. 'How could we
possibly leave him in the cave? And we can't drag him
about with us with all the animals there. Besides . . .' and
here an awful grin began to spread over her face '. . .
besides, he may still be useful.'

The Imp's heart leapt. So perhaps they weren't going to
kill him after all!

'How could he be useful?'

'Well,' she said, 'there are one or two nice little tortures
that I've always wanted to try out on somebody, but up
till now I've never had the chance.'

Tortures! The Imp gave a low moan of despair, which
would certainly have been heard by the others if it had
not been drowned by the shrill cries of the jackdaw.

'Tortures!' squawked this dreadful bird, jumping up
and down on the witch's shoulder. 'Tortures! Can I help
torture him? Can I snap at his nose? Can I bite at his
ears? Can I peck and peck and peck at his eyes?'

'Sweety-pie!' gurgled the witch. 'Of course you can
help. You can peck and peck to your heart's content, and
you're a good, bad, darling angel of a bird to have such
lovely wicked ideas. But I don't think we want to be too
hasty. If we go slow we can have much more fun.'

'What sort of fun?' demanded Sam . . . and his voice
was husky at the thought of all the pain he might inflict
on the poor little Imp.

'Oh – just fun,' she said. 'We could do a little roasting,
for instance. Holding him so close to the fire that he nearly
scorches, and then taking him out again and rolling him
in the snow. One might pass a very pleasant evening in
such a manner.'

'I'd say one might!' chortled Sam. 'What else?'

'Really,' she giggled, 'how you pick my brains! Well,
I've always thought how nice it'd be to take some horrid
little boy like this, and keep him in a cage with hardly
anything to eat, and then to sit outside the cage and have
the most beautiful dinner. While he was screaming for
food we'd all be eating meringues and peaches and turkey

and salted almonds and crystallized pineapple, and we'd show him every single thing we were having. Don't you think that would be enjoyable?'

'It's a swell idea,' said Sam, licking his lips. 'We'll put it into practice tomorrow night.'

'Tonight, you mean,' corrected the witch, pointing to the entrance. 'Look – it's sunrise!' And sure enough, the first red gleams of dawn were lighting the sky. 'Time we were making a move. There's a lot to do before they begin to arrive.'

'OK.' Sam strolled over to the Imp and bent down to study his face. 'The brat's asleep,' he said. As he spoke he raised his big boot to take a kick at him.

'Stop that!' cried the witch sharply. 'Let him go on sleeping. It'll save trouble.'

'I'd like to give him something to go on with,' growled Sam, grinding his boot into the floor.

'You can give him all you want when we come back,' retorted the witch. 'But first there's work to be done. Business before pleasure, that's what I always say.'

With a final grunt Sam turned away, and the next few minutes were filled with the bustle of departure. Not till the last moment did they unpack the dynamite.

'*You* can carry this,' said the witch, handing it to Sam.

'Thank you for nothing!' he snarled, retreating hastily. 'You can carry the stuff yourself.'

The witch glared at him, still holding the dynamite in her outstretched arms. 'If you don't take it this second I shall drop it on the floor.' And as though to prove that she were in earnest she dropped her hands a few inches.

'Steady on!' cried Sam. 'You'll blow us all sky-high!' Reluctantly he came forward. 'All right. Give it here!'

He grabbed the dynamite, and tucked it under his arm.

'And kindly be careful how you walk,' said the witch.

He did not reply, but shot her a glance of hatred. Then he walked out. A moment later the witch followed, with the jackdaw squawking on her shoulder.

The Imp was left alone.

As he heard the echo of their footsteps dying away in

the distance, a long sigh of relief escaped his lips. At least, for a little while he need have no fear of torture. But as he struggled into a sitting position, with an effort that made him gasp with pain, his heart sank even lower than before, for only a glance was needed to show him that no possible effort of his own could ever effect his escape.

This was the first time that he had had a real opportunity to study the way in which they had bound him, and it was plain that Sam had done the work all too well. His arms and legs were tightly trussed in a series of knots which only an expert could have tied, and the more he struggled the tighter they were drawn. Sam had not left a single loophole of escape. He was not even able to roll into a new position, for the strongest rope of all was tied under his arms, and fastened to a great iron ring in the wall.

'Help! Help!'

Feebly he raised his childish voice, but the echoes mocked him; it was so weak that it could hardly be heard even in the cave itself, let alone outside. Besides, who could there be, at this hour, to come to his aid? Every living creature on the Mountain was miles away, down in the valley, waiting outside the Treasure Trove . . . waiting to walk into the trap that would utterly destroy them. There was nobody who could help . . . nobody . . . nobody . . .

With a groan of despair he lay back and closed his eyes, giving himself up for lost.

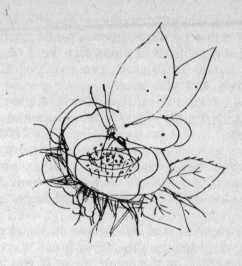

19. Birth of a Butterfly

But the Imp was wrong when he said that there was nobody who could possibly come to his aid.

There *was* somebody. True, it was a very tiny somebody – so tiny, and so humble, and so utterly unimportant that it is difficult to see how he could be of the least service to anybody, particularly at this late hour, when all seemed lost. However, even the tiniest creatures can sometimes play a great part, as we shall now observe.

Do you remember Mr Caterpillar? And do you remember how he was stolen, on the night that he turned into a chrysalis, and carried by the jackdaw to the witch's cave? And do you remember how angry the witch had been when she saw what the jackdaw had brought her, so that she threatened to throw the chrysalis into the fire? And how the jackdaw had saved it, and pushed it into a crack of the mantelpiece, intending to keep an eye on it in case it proved to be of any value?

Well, Mr Jackdaw *had* kept an eye on it for a while; but he had soon lost interest when he saw that nothing was happening. He had hoped that his little brown bean – for that was how he regarded it – would grow into some wonderful sort of fruit or some rich kind of nut that he could eat. But it didn't grow into anything at all; it just stayed brown and shrivelled.

'It's dead,' muttered Mr Jackdaw in disgust, giving it a sharp peck with his beak. For a moment he felt so annoyed with it that he thought he would bite it in half, out of sheer spite. If he had done so, our story might have had a very different ending. But just as his beak was poised to strike, the witch had called him, and he had fluttered away. And after that, he had forgotten all about it.

The days had drifted by, people had come and gone, and during all this time the chrysalis had stayed snug and warm in the crack on the mantelpiece. If you had chanced to peep into that crack, all you would have seen would have been this tiny brown case, that you might well have taken for a withered leaf or a scrap of crumpled paper. But you would have been wrong.

For that little brown object held a living soul. A tiny soul, but yet a brave one, who . . . at this very moment . . . was fighting towards the light.

Throughout the struggle between the Imp and the witch the caterpillar had been awaking. Through his closed lids he realized that the light was still there, and somehow it seemed to him to be gentler, more natural, like the sunshine he used to know before this nightmare began. Wearily he turned to one side, to ease his limbs, and to his astonishment he found that he could move quite easily, without hindrance. What had happened? Cautiously he began to raise his head . . . higher, higher . . . the cruel case of the chrysalis seemed to have disappeared. A wild thought swept through his brain. No . . . surely it was incredible . . . it would never be. Very slowly he opened his eyes . . .

It was true. He had Turned. He was a butterfly.

*

Mr Caterpillar – or as we must now call him – Mr Butterfly, lay very still, staring in bewilderment at the new creature which was himself. His first emotion was one of tremendous curiosity. What were those strange objects that jutted out from his head? (Humans, of course, call them antennae, but Mr Butterfly could not be expected to know that.) He supposed they must have been put there for some reason, but for the life of him he could not think what that reason could be.

Then he stared, with even greater curiosity, at his wings, which were lying folded by his side. And now, for the first time, Mr Caterpillar – or rather, Mr Butterfly – began to feel that perhaps there might be something to be said for being a butterfly after all. Never had he seen wings so beautiful a colour. They were of the palest blue and they were flecked with silver, as the petals of a hyacinth might be in the frost of the morning. Round the edges was a little yellow line, with here and there a speck of glowing green, as though he were embroidered in golden thread and sewn with emeralds.

Mr Butterfly's heart swelled with pride. True, he still had his misgivings. If this was to be his daily costume, it would take some living up to; one would feel as though one were always dressed for a party. And yet, it *was* his dress, was it not? It was his by rights, he had inherited it, and suffered a great deal for it; it wasn't as though he had hired it for the day. So he put aside his doubts, and after a few more moments they worried him no longer, for his wings seemed – as indeed they were – to be truly part of himself.

The awful question remained . . . would they work? Would he be able to fly? You may remember that this had always been Mr Butterfly's fear, in the old days when he had been a caterpillar. 'I have a horror of heights,' he used to say. And that horror was still with him. Very gingerly he moved his head and took a peep over the edge of the shelf. Oh dear . . . this was terrible! How high up he was! It was enough to make one's head swim. He swiftly looked away, and lay back, staring at the ceiling.

He was sure he would never do it.

And yet . . . supposing he could? How wonderful it would be, and what a lot of problems it would solve. For obviously, if he was to be a butterfly for the rest of his life, as seemed only too probable, it would be extremely difficult to avoid flying.

Mr Butterfly shook his head. He was afraid there was only one thing for it. He must make the attempt to fly. It would need a supreme effort; he would be scared out of his wits; and he would not be at all surprised if he simply dropped like a stone and crashed to death on the floor. All the same, he must do it. Better to die than to live for ever on the shelf, like a tragic cripple.

Very cautiously he began to lift his wings. Ooh! They were so stiff that they hurt terribly. He dropped them quickly, and paused for a moment's rest. He tried again; and now they moved more easily, so that he could hold them out and even manage a little flutter. He rested once more, and then for the third time he lifted them; and before he knew where he was they were quivering up and down, he was lifted off the ground, and was fluttering full tilt into the wall.

For a second he fell headlong and then, as though by magic, he righted himself. The little blue wings spread out straight and strong, and he fluttered this way and that, in a wild ecstasy of happiness. He flew from sunshine to shadow, and back to sunshine again . . . the whole world was full of sunshine.

And then, suddenly, he felt very tired indeed. And he fluttered down . . . down . . . down . . . to find a place to rest. Here it was. Something soft and gold, like a cushion. Gently he landed on it.

He had landed on the curly head of the Imp, who was just struggling back to consciousness.

*

Slowly the Imp raised his hand, and felt in his hair. As his fingers touched the butterfly, his heart gave a little

He had landed on the curly head of the Imp

jump of joy; here at least would be somebody who could share his loneliness, if only for a few minutes – somebody to whom he could pour out his troubles, and though it was obvious that such a tiny creature could not help him to get free, nor untie even the smallest of the knots that bound him, his very presence was a comfort.

Very carefully he took the butterfly between his fingers and set him on his knee.

'Where did you come from?' he asked, forcing his lips to a smile, to show that they were friends.

For answer the butterfly only gave a feeble flutter of his wings. He was still feeling too exhausted to speak.

'That's not much of an answer,' retorted the Imp. 'Who *are* you?'

The butterfly made a great effort. 'Mr Caterpillar,' he gasped. His voice was very high and faint, and it seemed to him as though it came out of the top of his head, for it was the first time that he had spoken since he became a butterfly, and he was not yet used to it.

'Well, well!' chuckled the Imp. 'That's very strange. You don't look at all like that to me. Are you sure that's your name?'

'Of course I'm sure,' returned the butterfly – and this time his voice sounded firmer, though it still seemed to be coming out of the top of his head. 'I'm Mr Caterpillar.'

The Imp's smile broadened. And then, all of a sudden, it faded from his face, and he stared at the butterfly with wide-opened eyes. Something in that high, squeaky voice seemed to bring back a memory, an echo of the past.

'You're not . . . you're not *the* Mr Caterpillar?' he whispered.

'Of course I am.'

'Princess Jill's Mr Caterpillar?'

'That's me.'

The Imp gave a sob of relief. Oh – this was wonderful . . . this was too good to be true! If this tiny creature had been sent from heaven he could not have been more welcome. He would be able to fly to Jack and Jill and give them a message.

And then, he remembered. It was all too late – too late. At this very moment they would be on their way to the Treasure Trove, to their own destruction. A groan of despair escaped him.

'What is it?' squeaked the butterfly, looking at him in astonishment. 'What is the matter?'

The Imp could not even answer; he could only shake his head hopelessly.

The butterfly blinked up at him, and as he blinked, his eyes – which were only just beginning to focus properly – noticed all sorts of things which had previously escaped his attention. For the first time he saw the ropes which bound the Imp hand and foot.

'Why – you're all tied up!' he gasped. And as he spoke he fluttered into the air and darted from one great knot to the other, touching them with the little antennae that sprouted from his head. He felt much stronger now, and when he came back to rest on the Imp's knee he was not even out of breath.

'Whatever has been going on?' he demanded.

'Oh, Mr Caterpillar – if you only understood!' sobbed the Imp.

*

Five minutes later Mr Butterfly *did* understand.

He could not even wait for the Imp to finish, but began to flutter violently round the room, squeaking . . . 'What shall we do? What shall we do?'

'What can *anybody* do?' The Imp shook his head hopelessly, for he was beyond thinking. 'If only I could break these ropes!' And he began to writhe and struggle once more.

'Stop!' cried the butterfly. 'It's no use doing that; you'll only tire yourself out.'

'I don't care if I do; I don't care if I kill myself. What does it matter? In a few hours we may all be killed. In a few hours *she* may be killed.' His voice broke, and a big tear began to roll down his cheek. 'Oh, please, *please* think of something, Mr Butterfly!'

Mr Butterfly closed his eyes and began to think very hard indeed.

'Are you sure that *everybody* will have gone to the Treasure Trove?'

'Absolutely everybody.'

'Mightn't there be one or two who were sick, or old, or something like that?'

'No. They'd get there somehow. Besides, what would be the use of anybody who was sick or old?'

The butterfly nodded violently, partly to show that he agreed, and partly because his antennae were getting hotter and hotter with all the thinking he was doing, and he wanted to cool them off.

Suddenly he stopped nodding. 'Wait a minute!' he squeaked. 'I believe there *would* be one person.'

'Who?'

'Mr Eagle!'

'Mr Eagle!' repeated the Imp – and there was a ring of excitement in his voice. 'Why, I'd forgotten all about him.'

'So had I. But I bet you anything that he won't have gone. He *couldn't* go. He'd get into the most awful trouble with the Mountain if he were to leave his post. You know what he always says to us about watching night and day – what a fuss he makes about it.'

'That's true enough,' agreed the Imp. 'Though whether he would have been able to resist the temptation to go . . .'

'Don't say that!' squeaked the butterfly. '*Please* don't say that, because he's our only chance. If we could only get hold of him he'd cut through those ropes of yours in a couple of minutes.'

'But how *can* we get hold of him?'

For answer the butterfly drew himself up to his full height of two inches, stretched his bright wings for an instant, and then folded them again. 'I will fly to him.'

For a moment the Imp did not reply. At any other time he might have felt tempted to laugh at the absurdity of the suggestion. So tiny a creature, a mere baby in the butterfly world, sitting there, on his knee, and calmly suggesting that he should set out on this long journey to the heights, against the winds and the storms and all the perils of the air – why, the thing was too ridiculous. From where he lay, the Imp could look out through the entrance to the cave up to the mountains far above; it was to those mountains that the butterfly would have to travel, on his thin, frail wings; why – the very thought of it was ridiculous; he would be tossed here and there like a withered leaf; he would be blown to destruction before he had finished a quarter of the journey.

And even if by some miracle he were able to reach his goal, how could he be sure, even then, that the eagle would be there? He *might* be there, it is true, but, again, he might not.

'What do you think?' squeaked the butterfly. 'Do you think I can do it?'

The Imp's eyes were clouded with tears, but he forced his lips to smile. No, he certainly did not think that the butterfly could do it. But how could he say that now? If he were to tell him what was passing through his mind, it would break his heart. Besides, what else was there? If he were to stay here, in the cave, what future was there for him? Either he would be caught by the witch, and crushed under her foot, or he would be left utterly alone in a world where all the rest had perished.

Better for him to make this one last effort, and die a clean, quick death up there in the mountains.

'Do you think I can do it?' repeated the butterfly, even more urgently.

'Yes,' lied the Imp, trying to make his voice sound as convincing as possible. 'I am sure you can do it.'

'Oh, thank you – thank you! I must start at once.'

'Good luck.'

'I shall need it.' The butterfly turned to face the entrance to the cave.

He took a deep breath, and opened his wings. The sunlight shone on them, so that he looked like a tiny blue aeroplane, just about to take off. Then he shot forward, and was gone. The last the Imp saw of him was a little flash of blue against the brighter blue of the skies he was setting out to conquer.

20. Mr Crow's Crowning Hour

A tear trickled down old Mr Crow's beak, hovered for a moment on the tip, like a dewdrop, and then fell with a plomp on to the blotting paper, where it made a little damp circle. A moment later it was followed by another tear, and as it rolled down, Mr Crow shifted his beak ever so slightly, in order to make it fall just to the right of the first circle. And when the third tear came he turned his beak once more, so that he had three little circles in a straight line.

'If I go on like this,' he sighed to himself, 'I shall soon have covered the whole sheet of blotting paper, and that will mean *more* trouble.' And the thought of more trouble was so depressing that two very large tears rolled down his beak at the same time, and fell in the same place on the blotting paper, which annoyed him acutely, as though he had been trying to cover a target and had fired two shots into the same hole.

He gave a loud sniff, puffed out his feathers, and lifted his head. He really must pull himself together. It was absurd, crying like this at his age. But then, it was his age that was the cause of the trouble; at least, that was what Mr Eagle had pretended when he had left him up here, all alone.

That Mr Eagle should have gone to the Trove at all was bad enough, after all the things he had been saying.

'I shall be at my post on the Great Day,' he had proclaimed, over and over again. 'No treasure for me! I must put duty first.'

'Never shall it be said that I left the Mountain unguarded in its Hour of Trial,' he had cried. And so on and so on.

True, Mr Crow had sometimes wondered, in the past few days, if Mr Eagle really *would* stick to his post when the time came; he had obviously been so very excited about all that was going on, and had been having the time of his life bossing everybody around. And so he had not been very surprised when Mr Eagle suddenly announced that he felt it was his duty to go after all.

What was so shocking was that in doing so he had calmly informed Mr Crow that *he* must stay behind.

'The excitement would be too much for you at your age, Mr Crow,' he had said. 'You must remain up here.'

Poor Mr Crow could hardly believe his ears. 'But Your Worship,' he had gasped, 'everybody else is going.'

'All the more reason why you should stay,' rejoined Mr Eagle. 'What would happen to business if everybody on the Mountain is in the Treasure Trove?'

'What sort of business *can* there be,' retorted Mr Crow 'if everybody is in the Trove?' Which, when you come to think of it, was a very reasonable question.

Mr Eagle glared at him. 'You are beginning to argue, Mr Crow, and it is not your place to argue. And now,' observed Mr Eagle, 'I really must be going. Heaven knows I do not *wish* to go.' He did not dare to meet Mr Crow's eye when he told this disgraceful fib. 'I would far rather remain quietly up here, attending to business. But I know where my duty lies. And it lies at the Trove.'

With which he stretched his wings, leapt from his perch, and was gone.

And that was why Mr Crow was sitting all alone, weeping on to the blotting paper. He sighed, and settled down on to his perch, staring out into the valley, which seemed strangely silent and deserted.

And then, all of a sudden, he began to blink. What was happening to his eyes? He seemed to have a speck in them, a funny little blue speck that fluttered up and down. He took off his glasses, wiped them, put them on again and blinked once more. The speck was still there. But now he saw that it was not in his eyes, but in the air, and that it came from a little blue butterfly fluttering feebly before him, as though it were trying to tell him something. But the effort was too great for it. Even as Mr Crow leant forward, the butterfly folded its wings, and fell senseless on the desk, in a tiny crumpled heap.

*

How long Mr Butterfly lay there we shall never know. To him it must have seemed an eternity, but it cannot have been so very long, because after a few gentle strokes from one of his softest feathers, which Mr Crow had hastily plucked from his wing, he began to revive and stammer out his story.

At first Mr Crow could not make out what the butterfly was trying to tell him, so feeble was his voice and so strange his story. But little by little, as the tiny creature grew stronger, Mr Crow caught words which made sense; 'the Imp . . . the Imp,' he kept on saying; and then: 'Danger . . . danger . . . the witch's cave'; and suddenly he realized that these stray words were fitting together into a hideous pattern, a pattern which at all costs he must understand.

As Mr Crow listened, he began to tremble. The moment that he had dreaded all his life had come, the moment when he would be left alone in a supreme crisis, faced with the need to take instant action. Alone indeed he was, for it was certain that he and the butterfly were the only creatures on the Mountain who were still at liberty. As for the crisis . . . it could hardly have been greater; it meant life or death to the whole living world. And he, Mr Crow, old and feeble and useless, was the only one who could deal with it.

Then, if you had been watching him very carefully, you would have noticed that a curious change began to creep over Mr Crow. He ceased to tremble, and instead of drooping down and staring at the blotting paper, he lifted his head and puffed out his chest. His eyes no longer blinked, but stayed wide open, and they seemed to have grown very clear and very sharp. It was as though this fearful danger had suddenly given him back his youth and the strength to meet it.

And that, indeed, was how he felt. 'I will show them!' he muttered to himself. 'I will show the whole world what I can do!' No longer did he pray for the return of Mr Eagle, to take this crushing burden from him; in fact, he would have been bitterly disappointed if Mr Eagle, by any chance, had come back. This was *his* moment, his crowning hour.

'Enough!' he cried, as the butterfly finished. 'There is not a second to lose! Stay here; I will return.'

He swooped outside, perched himself on a tall branch of the old oak that overhung the roof, and took a deep breath. And then, loud and long and clear, he gave the call of the crow.

'Caw! Caw! Caw!'

Three times it rang down the valley, echoing far and wide, as though it had been a trumpet sounded in battle. Which, of course, was what it was. For if ever a crow caws three times, it is a sign of desperate danger, and every crow for miles around must instantly rally to the rescue.

Would Mr Crow's call be answered? An awful doubt crept into his heart. Was he too late? Or was his voice too weak?

Once again he lifted his head.

'Caw! Caw! Caw!'

*

Now it so happened that by a stroke of supreme good fortune the Crow family, to whom Mr Crow was sending his passionate appeal, were at the very tail end of the long queue that was filing through the entrance to the Treasure Trove, far below. If Mr Crow had been only a few seconds later in sending out his triple caw, they would have been shut up inside with all the rest, with the doors which Sam had made slammed behind them. And then this story would have had a very different ending.

But fate had willed it otherwise. For just as they had been setting out for the Trove, the smallest Miss Crow, who was called Cora, and was always getting into trouble, swallowed a large red berry which she spied hanging on a neighbouring bush. As soon as she had swallowed it, she had a violent pain, and began to gasp and choke and cough, for it was a very poisonous berry which she had been strictly forbidden to touch. By the time that she had spluttered up the berry, and was better again, it was so late that her father had observed, in angry tones, that it was hardly worth going to the Trove at all. However, this had caused loud cries and lamentations from the rest of the family; so he had said that, very well, they would go, provided that they started that very minute, and flew fast and straight with no pauses on the way.

So here they were, a little breathless, but just in time.

'You very nearly missed it,' growled Sam, who was standing at the entrance, with his hand on the door.

'And that would have been a thousand pities, wouldn't it?' crooned the witch, who was standing by his side. 'What would poor little Cora have done if she hadn't got any of the beautiful treasure?'

'Shall I be able to have as much treasure as I want?' demanded Cora, in a somewhat husky caw, for her throat was still smarting from the effect of the berry.

'More than enough, my sweet,' rejoined the witch, all too truly.

Mrs Crow nudged her husband. 'Come along, dear,' she entreated. 'We are keeping them waiting.'

It was at that very moment that he heard the first of the three caws . . . far, far away.

Instantly he stiffened. 'Wait!'

'What *is* it, my dear? Why don't you move on?'

'I think I heard something.'

'Nonsense.' She tugged at him impatiently. 'Come along, come along. They want to shut the door.'

And indeed, Sam was already beginning to put his shoulder to the great door, preparing to lock them in.

'I cannot help that,' retorted Mr Crow. 'I am convinced that I heard something. Listen!'

He held out his claw to command silence. Mrs Crow and the three little crows stood there, scowling at him for being so tiresome. And then their expressions changed. For they too heard the call, faint but clear. And when a crow hears that call, he must obey it, whether he is old or young, or big or little. Even Cora knew *that*.

'I was right!' cried Mr Crow. And without a moment's hesitation he stood on tiptoe, and raised his voice in an answering call.

'Caw! Caw! Caw!'

It rang down the corridor, raising a thousand echoes, and the echoes had not died away before there was an echo in the sweep of seven pairs of wings. They were Mr Crow's seven brothers, who had been much further down the queue. They hovered above him, and the fluttering of their wings was like a wind in his face.

'What is it?' they demanded. 'What has happened?'

'It is the call. And it comes from outside.'

'You are certain?'

'How could I be deceived? We must go. There is not a moment to lose.'

Even as he spoke, a shadow fell over them, and the light began to grow dim. It was Sam, shutting the door.

He swooped to the entrance.

'Wait!' he cried. 'Do not shut the door for a moment!'

'What's that?' snarled Sam, scowling at him.

'Do not shut the door. We must get out.'

'Too late. Get back inside!'

Sam gave the door another push. There was now only just enough room to squeeze through.

Mr Crow made up his mind. Before Sam had a moment to protect himself, he flew full tilt at his nose, and seized it in his beak. There were a few seconds of wild confusion, filled with Sam's yells and the sweep of wings as the crows swept through the gap. Then, when he saw that all were through, he let go of Sam's nose, and darted after them. He was only just in time, for even as he passed through the door it slammed behind him, grazing the feathers of his tail.

21. The Final Battle

Would they never come?

For the hundredth time the Imp, lying there in the cave, asked himself that question, and for the hundredth time he cursed himself for doing so.

Through the entrance of the cave the Imp could see clearly; ragged black clouds were closing in from all sides; already the distant peaks were shrouded in a dark grey mist; the wind was rising, and moaning through the trees.

'The Mountain is angry,' thought the Imp. 'And He would be angrier still if He knew what was going to happen.'

If only he had told the Mountain before! If only he had run the risk of arousing His wrath, and had made the journey to the crater, and had shouted down into His depths! But then, the Mountain had always frightened him. He had never understood Him — He was just a strange distant spirit, whose orders he had to obey. He had never been a friend.

Of course, if he were to escape, it would be the Mountain who would save them all. On that matter the Imp's mind was quite clear. There was no other way out, at this late hour. All his plans were made, cut and dried. Over and over again he had rehearsed them, as he lay there.

If Mr Eagle were to come, and cut his ropes, he would rush like the wind to the secret entrance in the hill above the Trove, run down the winding corridors, take out his magic key and let loose the full torrent of the stream. By closing one of the doors he would divert the flow of the water so that instead of falling into the crater, as was its wont, it would roar back down the corridors, and pour out, in a mighty flood, into the great cave of the Treasure Trove itself. And if he were only in time, the waters would stream over the witch's stock of dynamite, and put it out of action.

Heaven knows, there were a thousand risks attached to this plan. Once he had closed the doors, and opened the flood gates, the water would rush down so swiftly that he himself might be caught in its toils. Then again, even if he escaped, he would have to fly like a bird to get back to the Trove, so that he could force open the doors with which the witch had shut them in; otherwise everybody inside would be drowned. And even if he managed to do these things, there would still be Sam and the witch to reckon with. They were powerful, desperate people; they would not give in without a fight – a fight to the death.

But what was the use of even thinking of these things? None of them would happen. Of that the Imp was convinced. The butterfly had been destroyed; Mr Eagle would never know; nobody would come to save him.

He heaved a deep sigh and shut his eyes, praying that if the end must come, it would come soon.

*

It seemed to the Imp that a dark cloud suddenly filled the

entrance to the cave, and that over his face there swept a swift breeze, and that in his ears there was the echo of many voices calling.

And then he realized that the crows had come, and that they were swooping down on the ropes that bound him, pecking at them with their sharp beaks.

Old Mr Crow, his eyes glistening with excitement and his chest bursting with pride, hopped on to his shoulder.

'Courage, Master Imp!' he panted. 'We'll soon have you out of this!'

'Thank you . . . thank you!' gasped the Imp. 'But I'm afraid it is too late.'

'It is never too late,' returned Mr Crow sharply. *He* was the master, now. *He* would show them! And over his shoulder he called out to the crows . . . 'Faster, faster! Peck away – peck away!'

A tiny speck of blue floated before the Imp's eyes.

'Mr Butterfly!' he gasped. 'You got there after all!'

'Yes, I got there,' squeaked the butterfly. 'But it was a near thing. And I shouldn't have got here at all if Mr Crow hadn't let me sit on his back on the way down.'

'It was a pleasure,' returned Mr Crow.

'Where is the Eagle?' demanded the Imp.

Mr Crow paused and cleared his throat: 'Mr Eagle,' he said, 'is elsewhere.'

'He went to the Trove after all?'

'He informed me that it was his duty to go.' Mr Crow cleared his throat once more and puffed out his chest. 'I shall have some words to say to Mr Eagle when we next meet.'

Having delivered himself of this very bold remark, he turned back to encourage the crows to fresh efforts. Peck! Peck! Peck! The Imp felt as though a hundred little drills were working on him. Suddenly, the first rope snapped. There was an excited cawing from the crows, and the Imp could now use one hand to help free himself. A moment later they had undone the knot round his ankles, so that he could move his legs. Then they all fluttered round the cruel cord that bound his neck. Peck! Peck!

'Courage, Master Imp! We'll soon have you out of this'

Peck! He could feel it giving way under the combined assault. One moment more . . . here it came . . . it had broken!

'You are free!' cried Mr Crow. 'You are free!'

The Imp nodded. But for a moment he lay there, with closed eyes and outstretched arms. He wanted one last moment in which to think. The crow family, panting with the effort they had made, and with little bits of rope still sticking to their beaks, stood watching him. Their green eyes were very bright, and very clear, and very trusting.

Quite still the Imp lay there. He was summoning up all his strength for the ordeal that lay ahead. He had barely half an hour in which to save himself, to save the Mountain, to save all the little world that he knew. Above all, to save Jill. Could he do it?

'Yes!'

He cried the word out loud. And though the crows did not know what he meant, they fluttered their wings and nodded to one another.

'Yes!' cried the Imp again. 'I can do it!'

With a single bound he leapt to his feet. So long had he been lying there, that as he stood up, he reeled and clutched the wall. But in a moment he had steadied himself.

Then, with a cry of 'Follow me!', he darted out into the open, into the gathering storm.

Up the steep Mountain side he rushed, with the crows dipping and whirling above him. The brambles tore his hands and caught at his knees, and the wind was now so fierce that there were times when it almost knocked him over, but still he flew on, as though the devil were behind him, as indeed he was.

At last! Here was the secret door which led to the Mountain's heart. In a sudden panic he clutched his shirt, fearing for a moment that the witch might have stolen his keys while he was sleeping. But no, they were still here — the silver key for the outer entrance, the golden key for the corridor, and the key of ice for the stream itself.

He pushed the key in the lock and the door swung open.

He turned and faced the crows.

'Wait!' he panted. 'I shall need you.'

They fluttered their wings to show that they were prepared for all that might come.

He turned again, and ran inside to release the stream.

*

A few minutes later as the Imp raced down the hill, he feared that at any moment the air might be rent by a gigantic explosion. And he had another fear – that underneath his feet, roaring along the secret caverns far below, the stream might be running so swiftly that it would outstrip him, and pour in a cruel torrent into the hall of the Treasure Trove before he could force open the doors.

On and on he raced, for what seemed an eternity, though in fact it could not have been more than a few minutes. And at last the goal was reached.

Never would the Imp forget that fateful moment when he plunged through the narrow gap that led to the dell, and climbed out on the other side.

The dell was deserted. After the storm outside everything seemed as still as the grave. There was no sound save the moaning of the wind in the cliffs above.

For a moment he stood there, panting, and staring in the direction of the great door that led to the Trove. Somewhere behind that door, as he well knew, were Jack and Jill and all the animals, and at any moment the waters of the stream would begin to pour in upon them.

But were Sam and the witch still inside with them?

His question was answered even as he asked it. Through a tiny gap, next to the door, scrambled two figures, covered with dust and drenched to the skin. There was no need to ask who they were, for even from this distance the Imp could see that a cloud of green smoke was hovering over the witch's head. They paused to brush themselves and shake the water from their clothes, and then

Sam flung himself against the door with his arms out-stretched, to make doubly sure that the animals would not burst it open before the dynamite exploded.

The Imp clenched his fists; now was the moment; come what may he must grapple with Sam and hurl him away from that door, so that he could open it before it was too late.

He shouted to the crows. 'You must deal with the witch. Leave Sam to me. Forward!'

Full tilt across the dell he charged, with the crows whirling and screaming above him. Sam and the witch were taken so completely by surprise that they hardly realized what was happening before the Imp was on them, and Sam was still standing against the door, gaping as though he had seen a ghost. Without a second's hesitation the Imp ran full tilt at him, lowering his head, and butted him with all his force in the waist. It was the cleverest thing he could have done; he was so much smaller than Sam that if he had tried to use his fists he would have been finished in a few seconds. As it was, Sam was winded, and staggered back with a howl of pain, tripping over a rock and landing flat on his back.

'First round to me!' gasped the Imp, flinging himself at the door, and tugging at the great iron handle, which was almost out of his reach. But it would not yield, how-ever hard he pulled. From the corner of his eye he could see the witch, in a dense cloud of green smoke, fighting off the crows, who were whirling angrily round her face, and he could also see the great wings of the jackdaw, who seemed to be fighting for his life with Mr Crow him-self. But still the door did not yield.

And now Sam had risen to his feet again, and was coming for him. He let go the handle and turned just in time, ducking almost to the ground as Sam charged. Sam's fists landed on the door itself, and once again he staggered back with a howl of pain. But this time he righted himself immediately, and came for the Imp once more; and now the Imp could not evade him; he felt the cruel grip of his hands round his throat; he gasped for breath . . .

And then there was a black cloud over his eyes, and a howl of rage in his ear, and Sam released him, for at that very moment Mr Crow had seen what was happening, and had darted to his rescue, sending his sharp beak straight into the fleshy part of Sam's nose.

Again the Imp struggled to the door. Sobbing with pain and half blinded with blood from the blows which Sam had dealt him, he flung himself at the great iron handle. 'Open! Open!' he cried, throwing the full force of his little body into a supreme effort. 'Open! Open!' Already great spurts of water were gushing through, proving that the flood must have reached the danger point, and from inside he could hear a shrill babble of cries and screams for help.

At last he could feel the door yielding ever so slightly, but as he turned to get a better grip, he saw a sight that froze his blood. Sam had old Mr Crow by the throat, and was choking him to death; his black limbs fluttered limply by his side, his beak gaped open, his eyes were half closed. With a cry of despair the Imp gave one last pull to the door, and flung himself to the rescue.

At that very instant the door gave way, and a vast flood of icy water leapt out with a roar like thunder. The Imp was knocked from his feet and tumbled over and over like a piece of driftwood.

Where Sam went he did not know; what happened to Mr Crow he was past caring. His eyes closed, and darkness swept over him.

*

'He's coming to.'

'No. He's fainted again.'

'Hold up his head. Let me lay it in my lap. There . . . that's better. Look, he's opening his eyes!'

It was Jill's voice, and it seemed to come from a great distance.

'Where am I?' whispered the Imp.

'It's all right, my dear. You're with friends. Lie still and rest.'

'Tell me! What has happened?' cried the Imp.

Jill pointed behind her. 'Look!'

The Imp blinked and stared about him. An astonishing scene met his eyes. Half the dell was flooded and turned into a lake, and though the waters were slowly sinking, the stream still poured through the doorway; after which it wound its way between the rocks, swept out through the narrow entrance, and then plunged once more into the valley.

'But where is Sam?' he gasped.

For answer Jill pointed to the entrance.

'He was carried away by the flood,' she whispered. 'He must have been swept right over the cliff.'

'And the witch?'

'She just went up in the air,' cried Jack, in an excited voice.

'What do you mean . . . went up in the air?'

'Just what I say. I was carried through the door on a great big wave, and suddenly I swept into a huge cloud of green smoke, and in the middle of it was the witch fighting with a lot of crows . . .'

'I saw her too,' interrupted Jill, 'and I was terribly frightened because I couldn't think where the smoke came from.'

'And then she gave an awful scream,' continued Jack, 'and just shot up into the air, like a big black bird. By the time the smoke had cleared away she had gone. Where do you think she went?'

The Imp shook his head. 'I don't know. But I'm pretty certain that we shall never see her again.'

For a moment there was silence, as the children thought of all the strange things that had been happening to them.

Then the Imp rose to his feet. 'Well, I must get busy. There's a lot to be done. And the first person I want to see is old Mr Crow. If it hadn't been for him we should none of us be here.' He held out his hand to Jill. 'Coming?'

But Jill only looked away.

'What's the matter?' demanded the Imp. 'Surely you want to thank him?'

'We can't thank him,' whispered Jack.

'Whatever are you talking about?' The Imp stared at Jack, and he noticed that a tear was trickling down his cheek. 'Can't thank him?' he repeated. 'I don't understand.'

'Oh,' cried Jill, in a broken voice, 'we didn't want to tell you, not yet. But . . . but . . .'

She pointed to a far corner of the dell. The Imp turned his head, and saw a group of animals, standing very still, staring at a little black figure that lay on the ground.

He was seized by an awful fear. 'Mr Crow!' he cried. 'Mr Crow!' And he began to run towards him.

*

The Imp pushed his way through the crowd. The animals gave way respectfully before him. Mr Eagle, who had been perched on an overhanging branch, fluttered towards him, but he waved him aside. He had no time for Mr Eagle just then.

He knelt down by the side of the little black figure. Mr Crow lay very still; his eyes were closed, and his wings were folded about him. It seemed, in some strange way, that he had shrunk; he looked such a little bird; so very small and so very frail; you could not have believed that only an hour ago he was fighting the storm on his strong black wings.

Very gently the Imp put out his hand and touched him. He was quite cold. And he knew that however long he held his hand there, no answering warmth could ever greet him, nor could there be even the feeblest beat from that brave little heart.

'Mr Crow!' he whispered. 'Mr Crow! I want to say thank you.'

But his eyes stayed closed, and his wings were very still.

It was over; he would never be able to thank him now. Mr Crow had flown far, far beyond his reach – to the distant fields and forests that stretch beyond the clouds, where the trees never die and the winds are still and there is peace for all birds, great or small.

'Goodbye, Mr Crow,' whispered the Imp.

Then he rose to his feet. There was another goodbye

for him to say, to Jack and Jill; he might as well say it now, and get it over. After that he could go away and weep alone.

He walked slowly back to the children, holding his head very high, trying to keep the tears from coming into his eyes.

'Well,' he said, 'I hear you're leaving us tomorrow, and going home.'

'Yes. We can't stay any longer.'

The Imp felt a lump rising in his throat, and however hard he swallowed he did not seem able to get rid of it.

'Then I suppose it must be goodbye,' he said.

He held out his hand to Jack, because he felt that it would be easier to say goodbye to him before he said goodbye to Jill.

Jack only stared at him in astonishment. 'What do you mean – goodbye? Where are you going?'

'I'm going home,' said the Imp – and added, rather bitterly, 'if you can call it home.'

'But aren't you coming home with us?' It was Jill speaking, and she was looking at him with a smile of encouragement.

'Home?' he breathed. '*Your* home? To the Royal Palace?'

'Well, it's the only home we've got,' retorted Jack.

'You can't mean it.'

'Why not? We've been talking about it for ages, haven't we, Jill?'

Jill smiled. 'Perhaps not quite for ages,' she said. 'But after you had saved us we both felt that we wanted you to be with us for ever.'

The Imp turned back to the children and held out his hands. 'I can't tell you what I feel,' he said in a trembling voice. 'I can only say thank you. And I'll come.'

*

They were interrupted by Mr Eagle, who had been hovering around for several minutes.

'This is a very melancholy occasion,' he said, with a

glance in the direction where Mr Crow was lying.

Jill nodded. 'Poor, darling Mr Crow. We were all so fond of him.'

Mr Eagle bowed his head. To tell the truth, he was feeling rather ashamed of himself. 'I have failed in my duty,' he said to himself. 'I have deserted my post. If I had only stayed outside and kept guard, these dreadful things would never have happened.' Which was not really quite true, for it would have needed a great deal more than Mr Eagle to cope with the cunning of Sam and the witch. However, that was how he felt about it, and he was determined to make amends.

'I was wondering,' he said, 'what we might do for poor Mr Crow.'

'What *can* we do . . . now that he has gone?'

'I had thought perhaps . . . a funeral?'

Jill said: 'Yes. I *do* think Mr Crow should have a funeral.'

'And so do I,' added Jack. 'The most beautiful funeral that anybody ever had.'

'And perhaps, as it was such a special occasion, you might be wearing your crowns?' asked Mr Eagle.

'Oh dear!' Jill gave a long sigh. She did not at all like the idea of wearing her crown, and she was sure that Jack didn't either but they agreed.

'Well,' Mr Eagle said at last, 'I do not think there is any more that we can do at the moment. I can count on you tomorrow?'

'We shall be there.'

'Shall we say four o'clock?'

'That will do very well.'

'Good night.'

'You are not coming with us?'

Mr Eagle shook his head. 'I think I shall stay down here for a little while, and sit with poor Mr Crow. It is growing dark, and he was always afraid of the dark. And though perhaps that does not matter now, I should not like to think that he was left alone.'

He bowed, turned, and swept slowly over to the other

side of the dell. He fluttered down by the side of the little body, which was now hardly visible in the fading light. And that was the last they saw of him, a black shape, keeping watch like a sentry on guard, covering his dead companion with his outstretched wings.

22. Farewell

The following day the sun rose, bright and strong. When Jill went outside the tent, after breakfast, she thought that she had never seen the Mountain look so beautiful as on this, their last day. All the hills and valleys were bathed in golden light, and though the winter was near, it was as warm as spring.

The Imp arrived at about noon, and they all munched their sandwiches together. They did not speak very much, for they were all feeling a little downcast at the thought of the approaching funeral. Apart from that, the Imp had something on his mind.

'A penny for your thoughts,' said Jill.

'It's my clothes,' said the Imp.

'What about them?'

'This is the only suit I've got. And I don't think it's at all the sort of thing one ought to wear at a Royal Palace.'

'But it's a lovely suit,' said Jack. 'It looks as if it were made out of fresh green leaves.'

'It *is* made out of fresh green leaves,' admitted the Imp. 'But they won't stay fresh for ever. Not down there. Up here, on the Mountain, it's different.'

'Yes,' agreed Jill. 'Everything's different up here.'

'That's what I'm afraid of,' sighed the Imp. 'I don't know whether I'll fit in.'

Jill shook her finger at him impatiently. 'Of course you'll fit in.'

'I don't know how to eat at table.'

'We'll teach you.'

'And I don't know how to say "Your Majesty".'

'That's silly, because you've just said it. Besides, you need hardly ever say it, except to Daddy sometimes, and then only when he's cross.'

'Oh, dear, is he often cross?'

'No, he isn't. But *I* shall be cross if you don't stop worrying.'

'So shall I,' agreed Jack. 'Because there's nothing to worry about.'

And then they told him about the puppies and the pigeons and the ponies, and all the animals that would be waiting to make friends with him. And they told him about the great fountain in the courtyard and the lake where he would be able to swim, and the grand staircase down which he would be able to slide. And they told him about Grannie Judy, who lived in a tree, and that cheered him up a great deal, because he felt that any palace where people lived in trees must be a pretty sensible sort of place.

'Perhaps I could live in a tree too?' he suggested. 'Perhaps we could all live in trees.'

'I don't think Mummy would like that very much,' said Jill. 'At least, not all the year round. But perhaps we might live in a tree some of the time. We shall see. Everything will be all right, once we get home.'

'Home!' The Imp whispered the word to himself, as though there was some magic in it, as indeed there is, to those who have never known what home can be. 'Home!'

he said again. Then he turned to Jill. 'Wherever you may go,' he said, 'it will mean home to me.'

*

And now came the time when they must go to pay their final tribute to Mr Crow. The funeral was being held in the dell, and as this was on their way home, they packed the final things in the cart, and clambered in.

As Moko started down the hill, with a jolt, Jill turned back and blew a kiss to the place where they had spent so many strange and happy hours.

'I wonder if we shall ever see it again,' she whispered.

When they reached the dell, all the animals on the Mountain were gathered around, but instead of the usual chorus of purrs and squeaks and twitters, there was an unbroken silence. As they walked slowly through the gap, wearing their crowns, with the Imp following close behind them, this silence was so intense that Jill could hear her own breathing.

Mr Eagle fluttered forward to meet them, and motioned them to a big log which had been rolled close to the grave. They sat down on it, still in silence, and then Mr Eagle flew away again, perched on the branch of an old cedar tree, and began his speech.

We will not try to tell you all that he said; it would be too sad, and we cannot linger for ever among sad things. But we shall just repeat the final sentences:

'And now,' he said, 'we will bid him a last farewell. We have no marble tomb in which to lay him, no stately monument to raise above his head. But before we go, let each of us lay on his grave some little tribute of remembrance. It may be only a flower, or a leaf, or even a blade of grass. It does not matter. If we lay it with love, and say a little prayer, it will help to cover him, and warm his heart, wherever he may be.'

He stopped speaking, and once again there was this deathly silence.

Who should be the first to go to the grave? Jill felt that it should be Mr Eagle, but he stayed quite still, staring straight ahead.

And then, from out of the shadow of one of the lowest branches of the tree, there fluttered a speck of blue. 'Mr Butterfly!' they all whispered to one another. 'Mr Butterfly!' And though he was such a tiny creature, so young and so frail, they all felt that it was right and proper that he should be the first. If it had not been for his heroic flight to the Mountain, in the teeth of the gale, none of them would be there at the moment; they would all have perished. Yes, they were glad that it was Mr Butterfly.

They watched him, fascinated, scarcely breathing. For a few moments he circled slowly over the grave, with the sunlight sparkling on his wings. And then he paused, quivering, and from his tiny arms there fluttered the petal of a red rose. Gently it floated down, to lie at last on the breast of Mr Crow, as though it had been the ribbon of some medal that he had won in battle.

That was the signal for the rest of them. The seven crows were the first to move; they stepped slowly forwards, holding in their beaks the wreath of holly, and after they had laid it over the grave, they bowed and stepped backwards, keeping their faces still towards their departed brother. After them came a whole host of animals, none of them crowding, nor squeaking, nor chattering, as they would normally have done, but all of them walking slowly, with their eyes to the ground.

The children were the last to go to the grave. And as they stood up, with all eyes on them, and the silence even tenser than it was before, a very strange thing happened. For the last rays of the dying sun sparkled on their crowns, and shed a golden shadow on the grave. Jill caught Jack's eye, and the same thought came to both of them . . . a thought so daring and so unexpected that they scarcely understood. All they knew was that there was only one thing for them to do; they must take off their crowns and lay them on Mr Crow's grave.

'Shall we?' whispered Jack.

Jill's lips scarcely moved, but he could see that she was

Lifted the crowns from their heads

saying 'Yes'. *Why* she said 'Yes' Jill could not have told you. They were royal crowns, studded with ancient jewels; they were worth a fortune, and they were part of the history of her country. How could she ever explain this strange feeling she had that it was right to surrender them, to leave them up here in the lonely mountain, by the grave of an old crow?

And yet, she knew that it *was* right. And she knew that when the time came, and when at last they reached home, she would be able to tell them, and they would understand.

Slowly they stepped forward. For a brief moment the Imp knelt down, tore a green leaf from his sleeve, pressed it to his lips, and laid it on the many-coloured pile. Then came the children.

Jill stood at the head of the grave, and Jack stood at the foot.

'Goodbye, Mr Crow,' whispered Jill.

'Goodbye, Mr Crow,' whispered Jack.

And then they held up their hands, lifted the crowns from their heads, and laid them, very gently, on the ground.

A long-drawn sigh echoed round the dell, breaking the silence . . . a sigh of wonder, and of gratitude.

The children stepped backwards, and stood there for a moment, quite still. The sun came out in a last blaze of glory, tinged with crimson as it began to sink behind the hills. It caught the gold and jewels of the crowns, so that they seemed like two little bonfires, burning bravely in the dusk.

'It is finished,' whispered Jill.

They turned to go. But even as they turned, all the animals began to move towards them, hopping and skipping and crawling and jumping and purring and squeaking and cooing and chattering. How they ever managed to scramble into the cart was a mystery, how Moko managed to start forward without trampling them underfoot was an even greater mystery.

But at last they were on their way. At the final corner,

they stopped the cart to wave goodbye. It was nearly dark, and the eyes of all the animals gleamed like a thousand tiny candles . . . yellow eyes, black eyes, green eyes, all lit with love.

Maybe, some day, we shall look into those eyes again.